As they got out of the elevator on the fourth floor, she wished her apartment was at the farthest end of the building

She needed time to decide what to do at her door, what to say. She hated the awkward moment of saying good-night at the end of a date. This hadn't been a date, but it had all the earmarks of one as they approached the louvered door of her dwelling.

Samara pushed her key into the lock and opened the door.

"Thank you, Justin," she said coolly.

She turned back, intent on telling him he could leave now that she was home safe, but she never got the chance.

She didn't know how she got in his arms, why she pressed her body against his or why her hands were on his forearms. She felt his warm breath on her mouth as they held their lips just inches apart from one another. Swallowing, Samara couldn't speak. Her heart leaped into her throat, pounding with the same force as a tornado swirling from sky to land. She lifted her head and looked into his eyes. When did they get to be so brown? And why did it feel so right to be in his arms?

Books by Shirley Hailstock

Kimani Romance

Wrong Dress, Right Guy
Nine Months with Thomas
The Right Wedding Gown

SHIRLEY HAILSTOCK

is an author of twenty novels and novellas. She has received numerous awards for her work, including a Holt Medallion, a Barclay Gold Award and a Waldenbooks award for bestselling romance. *Romantic Times BOOKreviews* presented her with a Career Achievement Award, and one of her books made the Top 100 Romances of the 20th Century list.

Shirley's books have appeared on Blackboard's and the *Library Journal*'s bestseller lists. Shirley lives in central New Jersey with her family and is a past president of Romance Writers of America.

Shirley loves to sew and bake, but she can't find the time to sew, and baking is way too fattening. She loves to hear from fans. You can e-mail her at shirley.hailstock@comcast.net or browse her Web site at www.geocities.com/shailstock.

The *Right* Wedding Gown

Shirley Hailstock

KIMANI™
ROMANCE

To my Aunt Carolyn
She always knew the right dress—
wedding or otherwise

KIMANI PRESS™

Recycling programs
for this product may
not exist in your area.

ISBN-13: 978-0-373-86119-4

THE RIGHT WEDDING GOWN

www.kimanipress.com

Printed in U.S.A.

Dear Reader,

The most common question a writer receives is, "Where did that idea come from?" In this case, it came from my love of weddings. Since I once worked in a bridal shop, I've seen countless gowns in just as many styles. I know the feeling of finding the most perfect gown in the world.

This is what happens to Samara when she buys an old trunk. What she finds inside helps to give her perspective and to understand that while it may sometimes make you vulnerable, love is also the greatest gift we can ever receive.

Justin Beckett has his own set of ideas about love, which keep getting in the way of him dating the girl of his dreams. But as we all know, love will find a way.

I hope you enjoy your time with Samara and Justin. I know I have.

Please feel free to contact me at shirley.hailstock@comcast.net or visit my Web site at www.geocities.com/shailstock.

Sincerely yours,

Shirley Hailstock

Prologue

Weddings and funerals bring out the absolute worst in families, Samara thought. And the Scott clan was no different. With the number of divorces and remarriages involved, multiple spouses increased the chaos exponentially. She and her sister, Cinnamon—the bride—share a father. Both sets of parents were present; Samara's father and mother, her father's ex-wife, Cinnamon's mother and her third husband from whom she was divorced, and all the noise that came with their approach. Samara had to give them credit, though. At least they waited until the bride and groom left before war broke out.

In Samara's experience, ex-wives and current wives

never liked each other. And that goes for ex-husbands and current ones, too. She could name several friends who were divorced and remarried. Yet, they couldn't be seated in the same room with their exes without a heavy atmosphere of hostility. Since neither of Cinnamon's parents were willing to stay away from their daughter's wedding, they were an argument in the making.

It started with a compliment. Samara's mother said how much she liked Cinnamon's mother's gown and Jordana Winston-Scott-Roberts-Newton took exception to her tone, reading it as an insult instead of the intended compliment.

Jordana proceeded to give her opinion of Mariette Scott's choice of a stepmother-of-the-bride's dress in colorful language. As they traded insults, all the while getting closer and closer to each, Samara could see an explosion was imminent.

She and Rena, another of the bridesmaids, moved at the same time, quelling the argument by stepping between the emerging front lines. The divorced third husband led Jordana away. Samara took her father off for a dance and Rena asked Samara's mother to help her with an adjustment to her gown that could only be done in the ladies' room.

The newlyweds, Samara's sister and her new brother-in-law, MacKenzie Grier, would be able to join in the laughter after the dust settled and tempers cooled when they returned from their honeymoon and people reviewed the day with them. They could howl over all the discussions and the arguments related to the wedding particulars. Since they were absent for the actual events, it would all have settled calmly in everyone's minds.

Samara looked around the room at the guests. They were smiling or huddled in groups discussing what had happened. Her mother returned a step ahead of Rena. She was more composed and Samara smiled at her as she approached.

Samara had plenty of role models. Her parents had never really loved each other. Her sister's mother was beyond her third husband. Most of Samara's friends were on the hunt for the second time. Despite this being a wedding, a ceremony that joined lives together, many of the guests were no longer sharing wedded bliss.

For Samara, the wedding and its aftermath only reinforced her conviction that divorce or unhappiness was inevitable.

She would *never* marry.

Chapter 1

The entrance to Shadow Walk was like going through the gates of Manderley. There was a dreamlike quality about the place that always came to mind when Samara Scott compared it to the opening paragraphs of *Rebecca*. The place had once been a country club that went bankrupt. It was bought for a song by her good friend Geri Muir. Geri restored the place, making it more glorious than it ever was. Shadow Walk housed a restaurant and several connected ballrooms. There were pro shops to support the golf course, tennis courts and indoor and outdoor swimming pools. On the property were several other buildings that Geri hadn't decided how to use.

Samara turned into the driveway. The road curved

around, winding through manicured trees and rhodo-dendrons. The last curve brought the main building into view. The architect intentionally set it far enough back so it would appear as a breathtaking surprise. A palatial structure, with a long front porch and heavy pillars, that could have been a Hollywood set. At night it was bathed in white light, making it even more dramatic.

The place had begun as a residence, then the property had been converted into the country club and Geri had added a wedding chapel and dining halls when she took it over five years ago.

Samara wasn't there for a wedding, instead, an antique auction was her reason. Handing her keys to the valet, she stepped out into the hot, July humidity and quickly entered the building. Carmen, one of her small circle of best friends, stood inside the door.

The two of them couldn't be more alike if they were sisters. If Carmen hadn't been born in Arizona and favored her parents, whom Samara had met, believing her friend was the product of Samara's philandering father wouldn't be a huge leap. They shared similar bone structure and facial shapes, but Carmen's eyes were a hazel brown while Samara's were dark brown. Samara stood a head taller than her friend. Carmen's hair was sandy-colored, reminding Samara of the deserts of the southwest, while her own was dark brown and flowed to her shoulders. Likewise, their skin colors complemented their hair, Carmen's light brown and Samara's a dark brandy shade.

"I thought you'd already be seated," Samara said as they hugged hello.

"I thought I'd better warn you first."

Samara stared at her. "Warn me about what?" Samara couldn't keep her body from stiffening.

"The person in the seat next to us."

Samara waited for her to go on. Finally, she asked. "Who is it?"

"Justin Beckett."

The name was like a whiplash cutting through her stomach. "Beckett?" Her voice rose a couple of notes. Then, realizing people were turning to stare at her, she spoke in a whisper. "What's he doing here?"

"I don't know."

"Can't we find different seats?"

Carmen spread her hands. "The place is packed. And these seats are assigned."

Samara knew that. Carmen loved antiques and since Samara worked with old documents, she was the one Carmen tapped to accompany her whenever there was a show she wanted to attend. Samara wanted to turn around and leave, but she knew Carmen lived for these types of shows and Samara wasn't about to let Justin Beckett drive her away.

"Let's go in," she said.

Carmen smiled with relief. "Atta girl."

Samara led. She knew that Carmen would try to take the seat next to Justin to save her the tension she felt whenever she and Justin were in the same room. She recognized the back of Justin's head and identified the two empty seats next to him. The surprise on his face when he saw her was evident. He stood up as she approached, surprise turning into a large smile. She did not return it.

"Samara," he greeted her. "I didn't expect to see you here."

"Justin," she said, managing to convey both greeting and dismissal in her tone. Taking her seat, she proceeded to ignore him.

"I would have sat there," Carmen whispered.

"I will not be intimidated by him," Samara whispered back.

The auction began immediately, which included several estate sales and Carmen was excited about them. The auctioneer announced the first item, a set of antique glassware. With enthusiasm, the roomful of people jumped right into the action as if this was the prize of the show.

As each item was brought in, introduced and bought, Carmen wasn't very active in her participation, although Samara could feel the excitement in her friend whenever something came up she liked.

"Is there something in particular you want?" Samara whispered.

Carmen pointed to an item in the catalog. It was a desk.

"You're only here for one item?"

"One I really want, but I like to see the other stuff and I'll bid if something strikes me as interesting."

Samara had been to several of these auctions. She watched with interest as item by item was sold to the highest bidder. She noticed the bright look of happiness on the winners' faces each time the gavel dropped and the award was made to someone.

Then a trunk was brought to the stage. "This is a mystery item," the auctioneer said. "The trunk was found in…"

Samara leaned toward Carmen. "I want that," she whispered.

"Why? It could have nothing in it."

"I know, but it could have old letters, documents, books, anything."

"All right," Carmen said.

Samara worked with old documents, but she wasn't a person living in an apartment full of antiques. A document could make her excited enough to wonder about the person who wrote it, the reason behind it, even research the history of it, but sitting at a hundred-year-old desk did nothing more for her than sitting at a desk made the day before.

Carmen acknowledged the first bid. There were few challenges and on the third bid, the trunk was hers.

"Congratulations," Justin said next to her.

Samara turned to nod at him. Then her attention went back to the auction. When the desk came up, the bidding was lively but mainly between Carmen and the man sitting next to Justin. After a moment, the man nodded at Carmen indicating his concession. The desk was hers. She smiled broadly.

Justin hadn't bid. He wasn't even looking at the items

or the auctioneer. Samara noticed that each time she glanced in his direction, Justin was staring at her.

Leaning toward him after enduring his scrutiny for twenty minutes, she whispered, "Justin, you can look somewhere else. I am not one of the pieces."

"I understand," he said. "You are *no* antique." His smile was more a smirk than anything else.

Samara cut her eyes at him and turned back to the auctioneer who pounded his hammer at the sale of a set of intricately carved ceramic tables. Why did she let Justin get under her skin? What had happened between them was years ago, when she first moved to the District. And before she knew what a jerk he could be.

When the program ended, Samara followed Carmen to collect the trunk.

"How are we going to get this to the van?" Samara asked, looking at her trunk. It had looked smaller on the stage, but now appeared gargantuan. She tested the weight by pulling on one of the handles. "It can't be empty. It weighs a ton."

Carmen had arranged for her desk to be shipped. The trunk would fit into her van so they agreed to take it with them. Samara knew both of them were anxious to find out the contents, even if Carmen had said it could be empty. From her test, Samara was sure there was something inside.

"Can we help you?" Justin said from behind her. Samara's back straightened at the sound of his voice. "I have a hand truck that opens to a flatbed."

"We don't need your help," Samara said quickly. "I'll get one of the guys to take it to the van."

They looked around. Everyone she saw was busy helping someone else.

"It's no bother," the man with Justin said. Samara noticed he was the man who'd been sitting next to Justin.

"This is my brother, Christian," Justin introduced him. "We call him Chris. He owns an antique shop."

"Thank you, Chris. I'm Carmen." She offered her hand and Chris shook it quickly, as did Justin.

"Let me get that for you," Chris said. He lifted the trunk and put it on the truck. In no time, he'd wheeled it to the van and slid it inside. Then the two women and two men stood awkwardly next to the vehicle.

"Since you obviously like antiques," Chris addressed Carmen, "I have a shop in Warrenton." He handed her a card. "If you're looking for something in particular, give me a call and I'll keep an eye out for it."

Carmen looked at the card and with a smile slipped it into her purse. "Thank you. I will."

"We should be going," Samara said.

Carmen nodded.

"It was good to meet you, Chris," Carmen said.

"Yes," Samara echoed. She said nothing to Justin, but nodded her acknowledgment.

"You were rather cold," Carmen said after the two of them pulled in front of Samara's apartment and were now angling the trunk into her living room.

"What?"

"To Justin and his brother. I know you and Justin don't get along, but you acted as if he didn't exist."

"He doesn't," Samara said. "Here's fine." She lowered her end of the trunk to the floor. Carmen did the same.

"He obviously wants to get to know you better, and you treat him as if he has the plague."

"As far as I'm concerned he does have it."

"How could anyone that gorgeous have the plague? Seriously, Samara, what's the history here? You never told any of us the full story." Carmen was looking at her with her lawyer-cross-examining-the-witness pose.

She was right. Samara hadn't ever told them the whole story about her and Justin. At the time she didn't know them that well. It had been a bad day and when she met the group for dinner, she didn't want to remember anything that had happened that day. They had a few drinks, she relaxed and Justin Beckett disappeared from her thoughts.

Samara sat down on the sofa. "I'd just come to Washington," she began. "I met Justin almost immediately. During lunch at the Stafford Cafeteria."

Carmen took a seat across from her. She frowned. "The Stafford? What were you doing there?"

"I didn't know much about places to eat and I didn't have all that much money until I got my first check. The Stafford gives you a substantial amount of food and it was good. I still go there occasionally." And she still saw Justin there, too.

"Too many tourists for my taste," Carmen said.

"I like watching the tourists sometimes," Samara confessed. "Anyway, Justin asked to sit at my table one day. I was reading a book and craved having someone to talk to. And there he was, this gorgeous man asking to sit with me."

She could still remember that day, looking up and seeing him for the first time. He had the most beautiful eyes, soft brown and able to render her speechless. She could only nod that it was all right for him to sit.

"He asked me out a few days later. I was alone, lonely, new to town and naive. I was ripe for him. He took me to a very upscale restaurant in Georgetown. We had no sooner been seated at our table when people started dropping by, saying hello. I thought he was an important man."

Samara stopped to look at her friend. "I suddenly imagined being on his arm at embassy parties and official Washington functions. You know, all the fantasies young women dream about before they move here and find they are as far from an embassy party as they are from home."

"You *were* naive." Carmen laughed.

"Yeah," Samara agreed. "It's the picture of Washington you get if you don't live here. Many of my friends at home still think I live like that. And it doesn't help to have a famous brother-in-law who actually *does* get invited to those functions."

"So what happened at the restaurant?" Carmen prompted.

Samara sighed. "A woman came to our table. She was as beautiful as Justin is gorgeous. And Justin choked when she stopped in front of us. She extended her hand to me. Her smile was wide and genuine. I took her hand as I'd done more than once that night, expecting her to introduce herself. She did. She was *Mrs.* Justin Beckett."

"He's married?" Carmen's eyes opened wide. "I didn't see a wedding band on his finger, but I knew that was coming."

"He's divorced now, but at the time he was still married," Samara explained.

"They were still living together, not separated?" Carmen asked.

"I don't know. I left right after her pronouncement and I refused to see Justin again."

"Good for you."

Samara knew she had done the right thing, but she found it hard to forget Justin. It took a lot of willpower not to let her eyes follow him around whenever she saw him. And he appeared to be everywhere she looked. Several times, after his divorce, he'd asked her out and she had refused him for a long time. She'd been out with several men since him, but none of them caused the amount of excitement in her that Justin had.

"Did you go out with him again?" Carmen asked. "After the divorce, I mean."

Carmen knew Samara's prejudices. "I finally said yes to one of his invitations."

"What happened?"

"It was actually Cinnamon's fault."

"Your sister?"

"She was here, looking for Mac. I suggested she call him, but she didn't have a cell number. I called Justin to get it and as a condition I had to go out with him."

"He must really be hot for you."

Samara frowned. "Well, it's one-sided."

"Meaning you've crossed him off the list of possible future husbands."

"Husbands? I am never going to marry."

"I've heard that song before, but why did Mr. Beckett get the ax?"

"We're just not compatible."

"Come on," Carmen coaxed. "There's more to it than that."

"Our second date, the first full one, went well. We spent a quiet evening in a small supper club in Georgetown. I chose the place, and there was no line of friends, colleagues or well-wishers drifting by to say hello."

Carmen nodded. "So it was the next one that changed your mind?"

"I don't know which one of our dates had been the worst. He was two hours late in showing up. I was breathing fire by then. I wanted to stay in my apartment, but he insisted we should go out. So we did." Samara took a moment to breathe. Her heart beat faster. She still remembered the humiliation of that night. "Neither of us had eaten, so we decided to just go and get something to eat. No first-class restaurant, just a small Italian place on Connecticut Avenue. We ordered and I was calming down when *she* showed up."

"She?"

"The wife. Now the ex-wife. The place was apparently somewhere they had frequented together. Justin was obviously surprised to see her. He nearly choked when he looked up and she was standing in front of our table. She asked to speak with him and the two left. Our meal came. I waited a while. Then I ate. Justin didn't come back."

"He left with her?"

"When I went outside his car was still in the lot, but he was nowhere to be seen."

"Do they have kids? Could there have been an accident?"

"No kids and if they had any, she could have called his cell phone. He was surprised to see her, so I don't think she knew he was there."

"What did he say when you saw him again?"

"The next time I saw him was at Cinnamon's wedding. And I tried my best to keep as far away from him as possible."

"He's never explained?"

"He tried, but what could he say? I had a cell phone. He could have called to say something came up. He could have called to say he was going to be two hours late. But he just let me wait, alone, in that restaurant that I didn't want to go to in the first place."

"And for an ex-wife," Carmen added. "That's the part that gets your goat. I'd be pissed, too."

Samara wouldn't address that. "They had been di-

vorced for one year, yet she shows up and off he goes.
I don't need anyone like that around," Samara said. "He
can take his attentions to some other woman. Maybe
his ex-wife."

Carmen sat back, apparently digesting the story
Samara had just given her. Samara smarted with the
pain and humiliation of Justin's treatment. Yet he was
still part of her makeup. As much as she tried, she
couldn't completely get him out of her mind.

Ignoring his phone calls and apology attempts had
kept Samara separated from him, but it hadn't quailed
her attraction. Sitting next to him for two hours at the
auction had been torture. Each time she looked at him,
she wanted to respond. To smile at him and watch the
crinkle around his eyes as he returned it.

"Why don't we forget the Justin Becketts of the
world?" Carmen suggested. "We can open a bottle of
wine and see what treasures are in the trunk."

Samara agreed with her. She got the dry Chardonnay
and two bowl-shaped wineglasses. As Carmen poured,
Samara got a hammer and pried the locks open.

She took the glass Carmen handed her and sipped the
dry wine. "Showtime," she said, sitting the glass on a
low table in front of the sofa.

Together they opened the lid. Samara gasped at what
she saw, backing away from it as if it were alive. Carmen
reached in and lifted it out.

"It's a wedding gown." Samara's voice was a breathy
whisper.

"What luck," Carmen said. "It's beautiful." She held it up, admiring it.

For a moment Samara couldn't speak. She stared at the dress. It was old, yellowed with age, but completely restorable and all its lace was still intact. The dress was made of a rich satin fabric. Its bodice crossed in the front and laid delicately in folds as did the skirt. Lace ran upward from the bust to the neck. The waist couldn't measure more than twenty inches and the only orna-mentation other than the draped folds that fell to the floor was a huge bow in the back with several layered strips that ended in a long train. It was the most beauti-ful thing Samara had ever seen.

"The lace is delicate and these tiny pearls must have been hand-sewn into the fabric," Carmen commented. "I'd say it was from the 1890s. Maybe earlier. What else is in there?"

Carmen laid the dress on the chair she'd been sitting on and looked into the trunk. The bottom was empty.

"Only this veil." She reached in and pulled it out. "Not even an invitation."

"Still," Carmen said, "you're lucky to find this. It's probably worth a lot of money. Of course, you could save it for your own wedding," Carmen sang in a teas-ing manner.

Samara laughed. "If it's waiting for me to put it on to walk down the aisle, it'll dry rot."

Carmen rolled her eyes. "Samara, you shouldn't be such a cynic."

"I'm not a cynic, I'm a realist." She turned and saw the gown. "I'll tell you what. You like antiques. I'll make you a present of the dress. You can wear it or display it."

Carmen picked up the gown and held it up to herself. She looked at Samara shaking her head. "I'm afraid it's no go for me. And it looks like it's the perfect fit for you."

Before Samara could stop her, Carmen had turned the dress around and placed it against her. Samara nearly overturned a chair jumping backward.

"Samara, you say you don't want to marry, then why worry about putting on the dress? You won't suddenly be a bride, would you?"

Samara hadn't thought of it like that. She tried to make logic out of the statement, but gave up. Her beliefs weren't steeped in logic. They were more like faith. She knew what she knew and wearing a wedding gown was something she never intended to do.

Samara's luck couldn't be any worse. First she ran into Justin Beckett and then the only interesting piece at the auction turns out to have a wedding gown in it, the last thing she wanted. She could dump both the dress and Beckett in that trunk and slam the lid closed.

By Monday morning Samara had put the contents of the trunk out of her mind. She'd done the same with Justin. She'd taken the dress from Carmen and stuffed it back in the trunk. After Carmen left, she'd pushed the offensive box against a wall and forgotten it. It was back to work, back to concrete things she could control.

Samara worked at the National Archives. She was an apprentice documentalist, someone who tested, verified and authenticated rare documents. Work required her complete concentration and Samara delved into it to the exclusion of all else. By noon her shoulders were cramped from bending over a California land grant from the mid-1800s. Suddenly she thought of the gown in her apartment. According to Carmen, the two shared the same time period. Samara had no idea where the trunk had come from or who had worn the gown. Letting her imagination take hold, she thought the dress and document could have a common history.

Smiling, Samara put the thought aside and went to lunch, then spent the majority of the afternoon with the same document. Most people didn't know that a documentalist could spend months with a single paper, trying to uncover its secrets. In this one the secrets would have to wait until a little later.

Going to the elevator, she rode up to the public floor. Her office was several levels below the public one, where the public was not permitted and most of them didn't know existed. The public floor usually calmed her. All that white marble should have given the place a cold, austere feeling. But the lighting was perfect. Done by experts, it softened the interior of the National Archives Building, bringing the heavy granite and limestone posts, staircases and high ceilings down to an intimate level.

Samara loved coming up here, to the public floors of

the building. She looked down into the case holding the Declaration of Independence. "When in the Course of human events..." She silently read the rest of the opening paragraph of the famous document that had established the United States.

Leaning over the case, her image superimposed over the words. Samara knew the history of her people, knew the hardships African-Americans had endured so she could stand here, the struggle they had maintained for equality, yet she felt a strange affinity to the documents in this room and other rooms not generally on the public tour.

The printing on the paper was faded and difficult to read, impossible in some places, yet it held the foundation of freedom for an entire country, a freedom that included her.

"Awesome, isn't it?"

Samara's body went taut. She recognized the voice. Justin Beckett.

She turned around. He was close enough to be a shadow and she smelled the cologne he wore. It was a light hint of a scent, pleasant, smoky, reminding her of the outdoors, the woods in Virginia where she'd spent many childhood summers and where her sister now lived.

"Justin, I'm beginning to think you're stalking me."

He smiled. "Not at all. I enjoy coming here." He ignored the sharpness of her voice and looked around the Rotunda. Only a few people milled about, looking up at the ceiling or down into the glass cases. It was nearly closing time and most of the tourists had left to get ready for dinner and whatever their plans were for the evening. There was a family of three looking at the inscriptions on the far wall, and the guards were at their stations, but for the most part, Samara and Justin had the place to themselves.

"Shouldn't you be at work?" Samara asked. She knew he worked at the OEO, Office of Emergency Operations, and it didn't matter that it was after five o'clock. When you worked for the government in jobs like his, there were no clocks.

"I needed to clear my head. This is a relaxing place and it's within walking distance."

The OEO was a secretive organization and not set up to handle disasters like hurricanes, earthquakes or blackouts. Instead, the lights at the OEO burned 24/7 and their purpose had international implications. Exactly what Justin did at OEO was unknown to her. The business inside its walls was rumored to report directly to the Oval Office. She'd learned not to ask too many questions when certain alphabetic groups were mentioned.

"How long does it take to clear your mind?" Samara asked. Her words had more meaning than were on the surface, but she didn't think Justin understood that.

"That depends," he answered, reminding her of a lawyer. Of course, Justin held a law degree, just like practically everyone in the District who worked for the government. Samara had considered going to law school, too, but she'd dropped the idea, preferring preservation and restoration to arguing the finer points of the Constitution.

"On what?" she asked.

"On you."

"Me? What do I have to do with this?"

"Why don't you have dinner with me tonight and I'll explain it?"

Samara was shaking her head before he finished the invitation. "I'm working late tonight."

"You can't work all the time. You still have to eat."

"I brought something with me."

"Good, I'll come over and we can eat your dinner."

Again she shook her head. "You know you have no clearance for where I work."

Justin's security clearance was probably higher than hers, but even with it, he wasn't permitted on the level she worked without a reason to be there. Plus, she was not allowed to have friends in her office, security was tight at all levels.

"And you're not allowed food or drink in that area," Justin told her. "We could eat right up the street." He pointed toward the wall. Outside, and only a few blocks away, were both the National Theater and Ford's Theater. Near them was an array of restaurants where theatergoers ate prior to the curtain going up. "I could make a reservation…"

"Justin," she interrupted him. "Give up. I'm busy."

She watched as his face fell a second before he recovered. "Maybe another day. You have to eat sometime. Maybe one day it will be with me." He turned and walked toward the exit.

"Don't count on it," she said, but not loud enough for him to hear.

If he could, Justin would kick himself down Pennsylvania Avenue as he walked back to the OEO. The air was perfumed with that combination of exhaust and humidity that was as much a part of Washington in the summer as the historic monuments that sat near any point of the city.

He knew he should have been up front with Samara about his marital status when he had first met her, but for some reason he wasn't, and she was determined to never give him another chance.

He should have moved on by now and he thought he had. Samara Scott wasn't the most beautiful woman in the world and he didn't kid himself into thinking there was only one woman on the planet for him. They'd had a few conversations and two eclipsed dates. Then a year ago, when he was having lunch with MacKenzie Grier, there Samara was, as radiant and beautiful as the first day he'd seen her.

But she had refused to have anything to do with him. And he couldn't really blame her. He cringed at the memory. He wasn't divorced at the time, but he and his wife were separated, although they were still occupying the same residence. Honora, called Honey by almost everyone, was Justin's ex-wife now, but on that night they were still married and she'd been especially angry. When she saw him with Samara, the situation was ripe for a collision and Justin was sorry the explosion happened with Samara as a witness. It took him a year after his divorce to get her to go out with him again. And Honey pulled another of her tricks.

Justin wanted to kick himself again for falling for her ploy. She didn't know they were going to be at the restaurant where he'd taken Samara for a quick meal. But he and Honey used to go there often. He should have steered clear of it, but he never expected that she would be there, too. She'd moved from the house they'd shared in Maryland to one inside the District's boundaries.

She said her car wouldn't start and she needed help. The gentleman in him wouldn't allow him to refuse. Outside, she said she really wanted to talk to him and would call the auto club. Borrowing his cell phone, since hers needed charging, Justin handed it to her. Honey was forever forgetting to put her phone on the charger and she could never find the car's unit. She got behind the steering wheel. Justin hesitated, but got in, too. The moment he closed the door, she threw his phone in the bushes, started the engine and drove away, taking him with her and leaving Samara alone in the restaurant.

"Take me back," he'd demanded, but she only laughed at him.

"So you can go with the woman who destroyed our marriage? Not on your life."

"Our marriage was over long before I met her. Now take me back."

Honey kept driving. Faster than she should have and it seemed as if the traffic worked with her. In no time she slipped into Rock Creek Park, where there were only a couple of stoplights from P Street to Virginia. When she finally stopped the car, Justin was well inside the border state with no phone. Naturally, Samara refused to see him again.

He'd tried to apologize many times, but all she did was hang up on him. Yet there was something about her that called to him. He wanted more than to apologize, he wanted to know her better. He wanted to find that something he thought he had had with Honora, but knew now was only a shadow of the real thing. And deep in his heart, he thought Samara might hold the secret.

Saturday, at the auction, when she had sat down next to him, Justin thought the universe had clicked into place. He made a decision to get her back.

All he needed now was a plan.

Chapter 2

Patchett's wasn't the best restaurant in the District of Columbia, but Carl the chef, outdid himself whenever Samara and her friends were there for a meal. Samara suspected he was trying to impress Geri. She owned Shadow Walk and it wouldn't hurt for her to know how well he could handle a kitchen.

The group had no set date to meet, eat and review the experiences of the day, but somehow the five of them were seated at Patchett's at least once a month. Well, four of them were seated. Diana was expected, but as usual, she was late. Of course, there was nothing extraordinary about that. Diana was always late.

The five of them had met in traffic school. Each had

be

lic opped for speeding and in order to keep their
Ove y had to appear for the eight-week course.
we ks, they each told their version of why they
spi e mandatory schooling. Their friendship
tua l class to a local coffeehouse and even-
past where they'd been meeting for the

D
ing

com d for a marketing and advertis-
at Ch tomac in the Crystal City
whic ined as a nurse and worked
haile e acquired Shadow Walk,
direct avor. Shane St. Pierre
was ar cording to her, she
her ow ater. Actually, she
lawyer up let her live in
office a men Icylin, a

All w h in its D.C.
married
wanted

cookies a

The c had been
no except hey all
his appear king
ways set h
of, Justin men
rebuff turned es that
arou ly. cheek, ti

"This has got to be the best Beef Borde of her
tasted," Carmen said, as she took a to the
meal, bringing Samara back to tho telling
Shrimp Imperial that she was when she got
didn't wait for Diana to orde himself to-
when she would arrive. S ." She looked
there.

"As usual," Sh t me. But it tastes
night. He mus of tonight's discus-
from Ger ach of them regaling
less the ng consoled when the

ut and then find out who
ggested in her usual log-

You've got another man on

eating. "Samara, there's a man
t brought him to the table?"
nding," Samara defended.

said. "He's gorgeous, with
could melt stone, a cute little
ght waist and buns of steel. I

just wanted to put my hands on them and squeeze," she said, grabbing the air.

The women squealed at her description and gestures.

"Unfortunately." Carmen glanced at Samara. "But he has a fatal flaw."

"What man doesn't?" Geri asked. The whole group at the table laughed.

"What's his flaw?" Shane asked.

"He's formerly married."

"Oh, my God!" Shane put her hands to her mouth, purposely overacting. "Divorced. Well, obviously he has no right to live. We should take him out and hang him." They all laughed. All except Samara.

"Give it a rest," Samara said, sourly. "I am not interested in him."

"Him? Does this *him* have a name?" Geri asked.

"His name is Justin Beckett. Works at OEO," Carmen supplied.

"Ooh, handsome and mysterious, too," Shane said.

"Yeah," Geri said. "Only a handful of people know what goes on in there. It's one of those agencies that never makes headlines, has an unpretentious address from which no one ever enters or leaves by the front door. And he has a brother who owns an antique shop. Maybe these two might have a mutual love for all things old," Geri teased.

Samara didn't like the teasing because it made her think of Justin Beckett all the more.

"Guys." Samara put her hands up. "Can we please talk about something else?"

"*I* have something to talk about." At that moment the always-late Diana slid into the empty chair waiting for her.

"Diana, where have you been?" Carmen asked.

She put her glittering left hand in the middle of the table, a smile splitting her face larger than Samara had ever seen.

"Is that real?" Geri ask incredulously, taking Diana's hand in hers and adjusting the ring to different angles to watch it sparkle.

"Engaged?" Shane asked, with awe and surprise in her voice. "When did this happen?"

"Today at lunch. Greg showed up out of the blue with a ring. In the middle of storyboards and marketing campaigns, he got down on one knee. I tell you, every woman in the office was drooling."

"And you kept this from us until now?" Shane feigned hurt.

"I haven't been separated from the man since. I could barely get away to come here."

They each looked at each other imagining what her words meant. A slow smile started on their faces and broke into a full grin.

"Congratulations," Samara said. She was happy for her friend. Diana had really wanted to get married.

"I am so happy for you," Shane said, getting up and hugging Diana. Tears were in her eyes when she straightened up. Using her fingertips, she wiped them away and resumed her seat.

"You have to tell us all the details," Geri said.

"Well, first of all, I want you all in the wedding," Diana began. "That includes you, Samara."

"Have you set a date yet?" Carmen asked.

"Next June if we can get all the details in place."

"Great, that'll give me time to lose some weight," Carmen said as she took another forkful of food and slid it into her mouth.

"I was thinking about the details on the way here. There is so much to do," Diana said. "If my mother was still alive, I could call her and then sit back and let her do all the work."

"Well, Samara has a wedding gown. You can start there."

Absolute silence covered the table as if all sound on earth had been ripped away. Four pairs of eyes were trained on Samara, boring into her with piercing directness. They all knew her superstitions about weddings. Samara didn't believe in tempting fate.

"Has something happened we should know about?" Geri broke the strained silence.

"No," Samara answered quickly.

"You were just protesting that this guy meant nothing to you. And you somehow got a wedding gown between our last dinner and tonight? What gives?" Geri asked.

"Guy? What guy?" Diana interjected, wanting to know. "Samara, have you found a man?"

"There is no guy," Samara objected. "You all act like I've never had a date."

"Well, when was the last time?" Shane asked with a laugh.

"Don't change the subject," Diana commanded. "I wanted to know about the guy."

"There's nothing to tell," Samara said, cutting her eyes at Carmen. She had turned this story into a drama. "Carmen took me to an auction at Shadow Walk and I bought a trunk." She stared at Geri as she emphasized the name of the place.

"Don't blame me," Geri said, her eyes wide and innocent. "I wasn't even there."

"Anyway," Samara continued. "There was a guy sitting next to me that I knew."

"Is he married?" Diana asked.

"That's irrelevant," Samara dismissed.

Silence hovered over the table again. Samara felt uncomfortable and needed to somehow steer the subject away from Justin Beckett.

"Anyway," she said, "when we got back to my apartment and opened the trunk, there was a wedding gown in it. I was hoping for old letters or books." She tried to downplay the gown, but remembering Carmen holding it up, she couldn't help thinking what she would look like dressed in the delicate lace concoction. Mentally shaking the image away, Samara remembered it was her sister who went in for trying on wedding gowns.

"So, you got a guy and a gown," Diana teased. She dangled her hand in Samara's face. "Maybe soon you'll have one of these, too. We could make it a double wedding."

"Dream on," Samara said. "Marriage is not part of my master plan."

"Plans change," Diana said.

The trouble with routine was you got used to it. When something changed, it could throw the whole day off. She didn't know why Justin had been coming to the Archives regularly, but he had. Samara was used to seeing him on her daily excursion from the bowels of the building. Even the guards would point him out when she stepped off the elevator. Now, it had been five whole days since she'd last seen him.

He usually surprised her in the main viewing room of the Archives building a couple times a week. But he hadn't appeared since the night of her dinner with her friends. It could be he was busy at work, she reasoned. After all, speculation was the OEO dealt with international emergencies and that could mean any number of things at any time of the day or night. There could be another reason, Samara's mind told her. Maybe he'd finally taken the hint and was no longer pursuing her.

Her heart felt as if a tiny pin had pricked it at that thought. She shook herself. Why was she spending time thinking of Justin? She didn't even like him. And after the way they had met, why would she ever allow him back in her life?

"She's right over there."

Samara heard the guard's voice and whirled around, thinking he was pointing her out. He was speaking to a tourist and pointing toward a child standing alone near a glass case. The mother's sneakers scrunched on the limestone and granite flooring as she paced quickly to her daughter.

Samara's heart dropped. She let a breath out. Good thing Diana wasn't here. She would swear Samara was disappointed that Justin has not appeared. She checked her watch. It was time to go anyway. She was meeting her sister for dinner and had just enough time to run downstairs and clear her desk and table before leaving for the night.

On her way to the elevator, she passed one of the guards, Alan Stackhouse, the same one who had pointed out the little girl to her mother. He was short and as round as he was tall, but he had clear blue eyes, a happy smile and a good word for everyone.

"Everything in order?" Alan asked her that several times a week. It always made Samara smile. The question and answer were a sort of game they played.

"Everything is exactly as it should be." She gave him the stock answer. She wondered what he would say if she varied the routine and said something different.

Here she usually got into the elevator and descended to her floor, three levels below. Today, she turned back to face him. Today she was varying the routine.

"Actually," she said, and then hesitated, "all is not the same."

His eyebrows went up in mock surprise. "Is one of the documents missing?"

"Nothing like that," she said. "It's not paper. It's just that I haven't seen Mr. Beckett in a few days. He's usually prowling around the floor, checking all the glass cases."

Alan looked up as if her words suddenly made him aware of Justin's absence. "I haven't seen Mr. Beckett, either, in the last few days. He's probably just working hard. Could be his busy period." The guard offered a solution to Justin's absence.

Samara nodded. "That's probably it," she agreed, seizing his suggestion as the truth.

The elevator doors opened and she stepped inside. "See you tomorrow," Samara said.

She wondered what was occupying Justin's time that he couldn't take a moment out for his evening routine.

Or who?

Cinnamon and MacKenzie had been married for a little over a year and, as her sister approached her, Samara saw she still had her newlywed glow. The smile she offered was as bright as daylight.

"You look great," Samara said as she hugged her sister under the restaurant canopy.

"Thank you. What about you?" Cinnamon moved back and studied Samara's face.

"I'm fine." Samara dropped her chin a little so her sister couldn't read her features. There was nothing really to read. "How's Mac?" She tried to change the subject.

"Mac's great. He's probably on camera about now." Cinnamon paused to check her watch and look up at the building across the street. "He's going to meet us when the broadcast is over."

Inside the maître d' showed them to the same table they always ate at when she met Cinnamon here. It was actually Mac's regular table and she supposed, being a celebrity, you get those kind of perks.

"Are you going to make me an aunt anytime soon?" Samara asked when they'd ordered.

"Are you going to give me a brother-in-law anytime soon?" she countered.

"Don't wait on that one," Samara told her. "You know I'm not planning to marry."

"I know you believe marriages don't last, but when you meet that one special guy, none of that will matter.

"Speaking of special guys, is there a new guy in your life?" Cinnamon asked.

Her sister always asked that question. Samara shook her head. "I suppose specials are out of fashion this year."

"What about an old guy then?" Cinnamon teased. "There's that guy that kept trying to get a date with you. The one we saw in Stafford Cafeteria. Did you ever go out with him?"

"I did not."

"He was kinda cute. What have you got against him?"

"Nothing. He's not my type."

"Shame, I just saw him."

"Justin!" Samara's head came up too fast and she spoke too quickly.

Cinnamon snapped her fingers. "That's his name. I've been trying to remember it, but I only saw him a few times and then only for a short while."

"Where did you see him?" Samara asked, fiddling with her water glass and trying not to appear too interested.

"Over at the studio. He was coming in to see Mac, just as I was leaving to come here." Mac was Samara's sister's husband. He was an anchor on the nightly news.

"Did he look all right?"

"What do you mean?" Cinnamon leaned forward. Her keen sense of intuition kicked in and Samara knew she'd played her hand. Although she denied it, she *was* interested in Justin.

"He looked a little tired, but other than that he was just as good-looking as he was the last time I saw him. Why do you ask?"

Several reasons she could have expressed went through her mind, but she rejected them all for the truth. "He often comes by the Archives. In the last few days, he hasn't been seen and I wondered if anything was wrong."

"So you *are* interested in him?" Cinnamon asked.

The waiter set their food in front of them and Samara waited until he was gone to answer. "Not really. It's just that I've gotten used to his presence."

"Has he asked you out?"

"Many times."

"And is that what you miss?"

"No, I miss nothing about him. It was just the routine that changed and I wondered why."

"You're not telling the truth, Samara."

"Why do you say that?"

"Because I know something you don't."

"And what would that be?" Her curiosity was peaked.

"I know you did go out with Justin and I know what happened."

Cinnamon raised her hand to stop Samara when she started to speak.

"He seems like a really nice man and he's interested in you. I know the beginning wasn't the best, but he is divorced now."

"Cinnamon, he was dishonest with me. How can I trust someone like that?"

"I don't know. I suppose you need a heart that forgives."

Samara stared at her sister. "What did he tell you happened between us?"

"He told Mac. He said you wouldn't answer the phone or talk to him. He said after finally getting you to go out with him, his ex-wife ruined it again. She lured him away—"

"Lured? It looked more like he was willing to go with her."

"She told him her car wouldn't start. Mac says he has a strong sense of honor."

"But what about the dishonest thing he did to me?"

"He told you the truth afterward and he was divorcing at the time. That part was true. And Mac says they don't come any more sincere than Justin. And as you should remember, Mac and I didn't have the most auspicious beginning. I was the one who was dishonest with him."

"That was harmless."

"You haven't been harmed. You're scared. I've seen it for a long time."

"Me? Scared? What have I got to be afraid of?" Samara's voice was higher than normal.

"Your heart." Cinnamon spoke quietly. "You feel something for Justin and you don't like it."

"You're wrong."

"It attacks your beliefs, your resolution that you'll never marry. Yet what you feel points you in his direction." She continued as if Samara hadn't said anything.

"You're wrong," Samara repeated.

"I know because I've been there, felt the same thing."

"This is different," Samara said. "I've seen him around the Archives. It's just his sudden disappearance that caused me concern. I'd feel the same about anyone who changed their routine."

"Well, it looks like you can find out why firsthand."

Samara looked up. She could feel her eyes growing wide in horror. Justin Beckett was weaving his way through the tables and coming straight for them.

"Justin," Cinnamon said the moment he reached them. "Please join us."

Samara wanted to kick her under the table.

"Thank you," he said, taking one of the empty chairs. "Good evening, Samara."

She nodded, her throat closed to speech. He did look tired as Cinnamon had told her. His eyes were strained and his smile was tight.

"I bring you a message," he said to Cinnamon. "Mac is going to be a little late. He asked if you could return to the studio once your dinner is over." Turning to Samara, he said, "He apologizes for missing seeing you, Samara, and asked me to see you home."

"That won't be necessary," Samara said. "I can take a taxi."

"Your brother-in-law has provided us a car as an apology. It would be an insult to refuse it."

Samara didn't have to look at her sister to realize this was a setup. Were both she and Mac playing match-maker? Well, it wasn't going to work.

Justin wasn't her type. Yet she wondered what had caused him to looked so tired.

Rain in Washington reminded Samara of the street paintings of Paris. The District had a similar version showing the capital's streets wet with the aftermath of rain. They made her feel as if everything had been washed clean, making the city ready for the next thing to come along.

Tonight that "next thing" was sitting beside her in a limousine—Justin Beckett. Samara maintained her air of silence although she felt the heat of his presence only inches from her.

"How long are you planning to keep punishing me?" Justin asked.

She stared at him. "Justin, what you did is unforgivable."

"I admit I should have told you from the beginning, but I knew you wouldn't go out with me. Today, I'm no longer married. And at the time I was formally separated."

"You were occupying the same house with your wife and who knows what else."

"It wasn't what you think." He smiled at her, probably remembering the happy times in his marriage. Samara didn't think there weren't happy times. They just didn't last.

"It was something you weren't willing to work at."

"You don't know that."

Although his voice was level, Samara felt the lethal quality behind it. She felt a little guilty for the flippant way she'd dismissed his marriage and his attempt at keeping it solid.

"You're right," she admitted. "I shouldn't have said that. I don't know anything about your marriage or why it ended."

"For the last time, please let me apologize for the way we began."

She hesitated, thinking over his request.

"I was telling the truth," he said. "We were separated and we are now divorced."

She took him at his word. But he was everything she didn't want in a man. Someone who couldn't commit for the long haul. So many people got divorced so quickly. Instead of trying to work out their problems, they just gave up.

Samara's parents, her friends, her colleagues were prime examples. Despite her sister's recent marriage and the bliss that lit up her face whenever she saw or even thought about her husband, marriage just didn't work. And it could get messy when you tried to dissolve it.

"Samara?" Justin called her back to the present. "We could start over."

"Why do you bother with me? There are so many women in this town. You can have your pick."

"You're beautiful, intelligent, people like you, and we have chemistry."

"Chemistry?" She stared at him, her eyes opening wide.

"Don't deny it. The first time we saw each other, you could feel the attraction between us."

"You're flattering yourself."

"Maybe," he said. He reached for her hand and slipped it into his. "But I don't think so."

Samara eased her hand free with as much finesse as Justin had taken it.

The limo stopped in front of her apartment building. The District was a collection of apartment buildings, row houses and classical monuments. The farther you got from the Capitol area, the apartments melted into single-family homes before the District blended into Maryland or

Virginia. Samara lived at the Majestic Apartments on Six-teenth Street, a beige-colored, pre-World War II building that had high ceilings, louvered doors and large rooms. Her building hadn't been cut up into tiny bits of square footage to accommodate more people and allow the management to collect more rent. On good days she could walk to the White House and the Archives a little farther away.

The driver opened the door and she scrambled out. Justin followed her. Samara turned on the sidewalk and stared at him.

"I'll be fine from here," she said. She wanted to be rid of him.

"I'll see you to your door," Justin stated as if he wasn't willing to negotiate the point.

"This is a protected building. I'll be fine." Her build-ing had a guard at the door and you had to be announced or known in order to get past the locked doors.

"I'll see you to your door," Justin repeated.

Samara looked at the lighted doorway and went up the three steps to the landing. Between the landing and the double doors that led to the lobby was a long strip of concrete flanked by manicured hedges. Justin put his hand on her elbow and fell into step beside her. Samara felt the warmth of his hand.

She walked straight toward the entrance, but wondered how she could do it. For some reason she didn't under-stand, him holding her felt both strange and wonderful. Samara wanted to move her arm across herself and link hands with him. But she didn't. She continued to the entrance and straight to the elevator, not even acknowledging the night clerk whom she always smiled at and had a few words with before going up to her apartment.

As they got out of the elevator on the fourth floor, she wished her apartment was at the farthest end of the building. She needed time to decide what to do at her door, what to say. She had the awkward moment of saying good-night at the end of a date. This hadn't been a date, but it had all the earmarks of one as they approached the louvered door of her domain.

Samara pushed her key in the lock and opened the door. "Thank you, Justin." She turned back intent on telling him she was safely home and he could leave now, but she never got the chance.

She didn't know how she got in his arms, or why his body was pressed against hers, why her hands were on his forearms. His breath fanned her mouth. Swallowing, Samara couldn't speak. Her heart leaped into her throat, pounding with the same force as a tornado swirling from sky to land. She lifted her head and looked into his eyes. When did they get to be so brown? And why did it feel so right to be in his arms?

"Just—" she started, but Justin covered her mouth again. Samara submitted without resistance. Holding her, he had taken her resistance away. His mouth was strong, determined, insistent. Samara opened hers and his tongue swept inside. Laser-sharp sensations slashed into her body, attached themselves to erogenous nerve endings and let the need in her flow freely.

Her body acted on its own. Her feet pushed her up on her toes and her arms curled around Justin's neck as she joined him in a kiss that was rapidly turning desperate. Waves of pleasure Samara had never felt before coursed through her. Heat inched up from her toes, then burst through her body, suffusing it like a suddenly opened furnace.

Justin's hands caressed her back. Heat followed their movement to the point Samara thought she'd melt under his touch.

Sliding her mouth free, she gasped for air, her body so weak that only Justin's arms were keeping her upright. Resting her head on his shoulder, Samara was trying to get her breathing under control, trying to make sense of what had happened, while still being enclosed in an embrace that had her craving more. She'd never experienced anything like that. It was a kiss. It's not like she hadn't been kissed before, but she felt as if she hadn't. She'd never been so thoroughly, desperately wanted and aroused that she felt the communication from his mouth through her entire body. Never been so well-kissed that she had no ability to hold herself erect.

"See what I mean about chemistry?" he asked, his voice scratchy and lower than normal.

"Oh, yeah," Samara said. "I think I know all about chemistry now."

Chapter 3

Samara was avoiding him. Justin knew she would do that. He'd known as he had walked back to the elevator that took him to the main floor and out to the waiting limousine. The kiss had been the capstone of the night. It was natural. He hadn't planned it, but she looked so beautiful. He'd been thinking of it all night. When she turned, he knew she was about to leave him. His arms were around her waist before he'd thought of putting them there.

And now she was retaliating.

Justin stared down into the Declaration of Independence case. Samara seemed to prefer this part of the Archives. When he found her in the Rotunda, she was usually here. But he'd come to the Archives every night since his impromptu drive to her apartment and the subsequent good-night kiss, and Samara had yet to appear.

He knew she had to exit the building on the street level. There were several exits other than the one the employees used. Unfortunately, there was a subway stop only a few steps from where Samara worked. She could easily leave and disappear without him seeing her.

Justin had looked for her on the street, had followed the movements of total strangers when he thought he had seen her. He'd been in the Rotunda for an hour. Samara wasn't here and he didn't expect she would come.

Leaving the building, he turned quickly and nearly walked into someone.

"Excuse me," he said, his arms coming out to keep them both steady. "Samara," he said, surprised to find the object of his thoughts.

She stepped back out of his arms. "I want to talk to you," she said.

"I thought you were avoiding me."

"I've been very busy. We have an exhibit going on tour and cleaning and getting it ready to leave the building is a major undertaking."

"Let's go somewhere and have a drink." He didn't give her time to refuse. Taking her arm, he pulled her down the steps and into a waiting taxi. Moments later they were seated in a secluded booth, hugging glasses of white wine.

"What was in the trunk?" he asked.

They weren't here to discuss the auction, but bringing up the kiss was something she wasn't ready to do right at the moment. Maybe he wasn't either and that's why he asked about the trunk.

"There wasn't much in it."

"You were hoping for what?"

"Old books, letters, diaries, documents."

"And it was empty?"

"There was a dress in it."

"That's all? It was a large trunk to only hold one dress."

"It was large dress. A wedding dress."

"Oh," he said. "Did it fit?"

The smile on his face told her he knew the story of her sister trying on a wedding gown that didn't belong to her.

"I'm not Cinnamon. I would never do such a thing."

"I thought women loved to try on clothes."

"Clothes, yes. The ones they intend to buy. Not another woman's clothes." She frowned, knowing in high school she had exchanged clothes with her friends all the time. And she and Cinnamon had also worn each other's clothes when they visited each other. But she was no longer sixteen.

Samara took a sip of her wine. Justin was staring into her face. He had a Cheshire-cat smile on his face.

"What's so funny?" she asked.

"It's not funny," he said. "I was imagining how you'd look in a wedding gown."

"We won't be finding out because I'm never going to wear one."

"Why not? Are you the navy-blue-suit type? Or don't you ever intend to marry?"

"No, I do not," she said in a voice that sounded as if it was right out of the Victorian period.

Justin smiled. "There's a challenge if I've ever heard one."

"It's not a challenge," Samara argued. "I don't accept challenges. I simply stated a fact."

"You'll change your mind when you meet the right man."

Samara dropped her chin so Justin couldn't see her roll her eyes. She'd heard that litany from everyone.

"You know statistics don't put faith in the 'till death do us part' stuff."

"I know what the current stats are." He paused and Samara remembered he was one of the statistics. "But the divorce rate doesn't stop people from trying or from falling in love."

"Love makes them blind," she told him. "And not *only* blind. Like teenage hormones, it makes you crazy, too. But hormones eventually settle down and you return to normal with not much harm. Love can make you crazy for life."

"Samara," he said, surprised at her words. "You're a cynic."

"I prefer to think of myself as a realist." She stared him directly in the eye. "What are *you?* One of those people who thinks he'll find the perfect woman, wife and mother of his children?"

He nodded his head slowly. "I think I've already found her."

Samara smiled widely. That was wonderful news. Now maybe he would leave her alone.

"Great," she told him. "Who is the lucky lady?"

"You."

Samara's mouth dropped open and her wineglass slipped from her fingers.

The day was a waste of time. Why Samara chose to go to work was a mystery. She should have stayed in bed. But she'd told herself that Justin's little bombshell from the night before would not bother her in the least.

But it did.

She'd thought of nothing else, even when she was working on the sensitive paper of the Red Letters. "Red Letters" was a name she and her colleagues had given to a collection that had been donated to the Archives. The letters were more than one hundred years old and written on paper that was red. They were between a woman and her fiancé, covering several years of separation.

He was in Colorado and she'd been left in the District. The letters reported the day-to-day life of an affluent woman and chronicled everything from the popularity of the bicycle to the marriage of President Grover Cleveland. The family had donated them after finding them hidden in a spring-locking drawer of a piece of antique furniture.

Normally, this kind of thing would block out any

other thoughts, but today Samara couldn't get Justin out of her head.

She was thankful it was time to go. And also thankful she had a diversion. Geri called earlier in the day and insisted she come to Shadow Walk after work. She said she had wonderful news. Samara didn't try to figure out what it was. Her mind was selfish and only interested in her own problems at the moment.

"Samara."

She turned at the sound of her name. Alan Stackhouse stopped her at the elevator. She didn't usually see him on this level and it surprised her.

"What are you doing here?" she asked, looking around in case anyone else saw them.

"I have something for you." He handed her an envelope. It was plain white, nondescript, with her first name printed in heavy, dark block letters.

"Who's it from?" she asked.

"Open it," he responded. Then he walked away with a knowing smile on his face.

The elevator doors opened and for a moment, Samara stood there deciding whether to get on or follow the guard. Stepping inside, she looked at the envelope as the doors closed and the small room lifted toward the street level.

Turning the envelope over, she found it wasn't sealed. The doors opened and she stepped out onto the granite and limestone flooring. There was a crowd heading toward the exit and she was in the middle of it. She smiled to herself as she walked outside.

The heat hit her like a wash of volcanic lava. Putting the envelope in her purse, she hurried for the subway and the blessed coolness of air-conditioning. She imagined a secret admirer, and wanted to open the envelope in a private place, without the prying eyes of whoever was sitting next to her on the ride to her apartment.

She needed her car to get to Shadow Walk and it was parked in the space allotted her under her apartment building. The letter would have to wait.

Taking the time to quickly change out of her work clothes and put on a short cotton shirt and a pair of pants, Samara rushed out the door and off to Shadow Walk.

"You're late," Diana accused as Samara walked into Geri's office. Samara had passed the main salon, as Geri called her halls. It wasn't in use, but there were people being shown around who were planning a wedding. Samara assumed Diana's reception would take place at Shadow Walk.

"You are the last person in the world who should point at someone who's late." Samara stared at her.

"The rest of us have been waiting for nearly an hour and Geri won't tell us anything about why we're here."

Looking at Geri, Samara also wondered what the reason was for her calling them together. They were friends, good friends, the kind of friends you could call at a moment's notice and have them come to your aid whether it was breakfast time or the middle of the night.

"Well, Geri, what's the story?" Samara asked.

"Come with me. I'll show you."

They left the office as if they were members of a parade. Geri passed familiar rooms that the five of them had been in many times. Samara glanced into the room where the auction had taken place. Justin's face came to mind as quickly. She saw the room as it had been set up that day, with seating and a one-step stage. Although it was empty of everything except the essence of memory, she felt as if Justin had just looked over his shoulder and smiled at her standing in the doorway.

"Don't dawdle, Samara," Shane said.

Samara rejoined them. Geri passed the dining hall. The din rose and fell from people enjoying their evening meal. She continued to the door at the side of the building. Then went through it and out into the heat of the setting sun.

"Where are we going?" Diana asked.

"Right over here." Geri stopped in front of a small building. It had housed the gift shop, but Geri had relocated that within the main building. Sales increased three hundred percent in the first month of the move.

Opening the door, she went inside. The group followed her. The air was thick and stuffy.

"What is this?" Shane asked.

"My new bridal shop," Geri announced as if she'd just given birth. "We have so many weddings here, why not a bridal shop? This way the brides can have a full package."

"One-stop shopping," Shane said flatly.

"You don't think it's a good idea?"

"I do," Diana said. "I love going to one place and being able to do everything without driving all over the place."

"What do you think, Samara?" Geri addressed her.

"I think you're an astute business woman and if you think this will succeed, then it will," she answered.

"That was diplomatic," Carmen chimed in.

"Geri, you're spread thin right now." Samara ignored Carmen. "Do you think you have time for a new venture?"

"That's the beauty of it. I'm hiring a manager."

"Who?"

"Whom," she corrected.

"All right, whom?" Carmen shouted.

"My mother."

"What?" Shane and Diana spoke at the same time.

"She's divorced and at her wit's end. She needs something to do. Plus, she's good with people. This will be perfect for her."

"Geri, has she ever dealt directly with the public?" asked Samara.

Geri shook her head.

"What about her job? Isn't she still working in that tax office?" asked Shane.

"She isn't in tax. She's in financial analysis and she says she's tired of it. She wants to do something different."

"This feels like a midlife crisis to me," Diana said.

"There's probably some of that," Geri admitted. "The divorce hit her hard. She needs something to concentrate on."

"Do you think she'll be happy here?" Samara asked.

"She's only been divorced a few months. A bridal shop, with all the tearfully happy brides, could depress her."

"She promised she'd tell me if she didn't think she could do it."

"Well, I'm behind it then," Samara said.

"I knew you would be," Shane stated matter-of-factly. Then she looked at Geri. "I'm with you," she said.

Geri looked at her other two friends who nodded their assent.

"Great!" she said as she smiled, and embraced them in a group hug. "Now that that's settled," Geri continued, then backed away from the group, "I need your help."

"Sure," said Shane.

"What?" Carmen asked. They could all hear the skepticism in her voice.

"We thought we'd open with a huge fashion show."

"Oh, good idea," Carmen said.

"Something big," Geri elaborated. "We'll advertise it all over the place, Internet, local radio, area bridal shops, even to the customers here."

"And you want me to try to get someone from the television station to do a story on the opening?" Samara knew this was the help Geri wanted.

"Thank you, but I wouldn't ask that," Geri said, surprising all four women.

"You have to do that," the group almost spoke as one.

"Don't worry, Geri," Samara eclipsed the discussion. "I'll ask Mac if he can do anything."

Geri rushed over and hugged her. "That would be wonderful." Turning back to the group. "But that's not all."

"What more do you want?" Shane asked. "Diana will buy her gown here."

"Sure I will," Diana agreed. "I can be your first customer."

"Thanks, but that's not it, either." She paused, taking the time to look at each one of them before she spoke. "I want you all to be models in the fashion show and wear the gowns."

"No way," Samara said, taking a step back as if Geri's words could physically attack her. "No way am I putting on a wedding gown."

For the second time in two days, Samara was doing something she'd told herself she wouldn't do. Last night she'd sworn she wouldn't be in Geri's fashion show. But she let herself be talked into it. Now she was committed.

But only as a bridesmaid.

After her agreement, Geri and her other friends seemed to run amok with plans. Diana put on her marketing hat and suggested a television campaign. While it was well out of Geri's budget, they all jumped on the bandwagon. Shane suggested placing ads in the playbills used in the theater. Geri took it a step further and suggested an all-out, national, print-media campaign. They all laughed, but the action didn't stop. Ideas were being thrown about like candy pouring from a piñata. Samara couldn't resist getting into the fray. Planning was fun. So much so that Samara forgot about the letter the guard had given her before she left work.

The envelope fell out of her pocket the next morning when Samara picked up her jacket from where she'd dropped it the night before. She opened the flap and pulled a postcard out. The photo was vintage. It was a picture of a restaurant. Samara recognized it as a place in Georgetown near Key Bridge.

On the back was a date and time. Nothing else. She turned it over several times, but nothing more appeared. She looked at the photo. After a moment she laughed. This had to be Justin's idea, a reply to her *challenge*.

Eight o'clock, it read. And the date was tonight. She laughed, thinking there was no way she was going to meet him. Just like she wasn't wearing a wedding gown in a fashion show, she reminded herself.

As she turned, she saw the trunk and regretted that she hadn't had it moved to storage. She approached it slowly. For Geri and Diana's sake, she lifted the lid, the white lace gown staring back at her like an angel that had fallen from heaven. She picked up the dress and held it by the sleeves, looking at the fine detailed work that some loving hand had spent days completing. Samara wondered what had that long-ago seamstress thought as she worked her art into the dress.

Samara went to a long mirror and looked at the dress as she held it against herself. Stretching her arm out, she admired the mutton sleeves. She liked the look, had admired them in many late-night movies made in the '30s and '40s. Of course, most of the actresses wearing them had perfect posture. Samara stood up taller at the thought.

The lace as Carmen had said had hand-sewn pearls in it and was fully intact. But what Samara really liked was the way the satin folds draped to the floor and the large bow that ended in a train.

Many women had gowns cut down to a shorter length. She could do that and it would no longer be a wedding gown. But as she saw herself in the mirror, she knew there was no way she'd be able to cut the dress. It was too beautiful.

And it looked as if it was her size.

All day she'd thought about the invitation. All day she'd told herself she wasn't going to meet Justin. They had nothing in common. There was no reason for her to respond. It wasn't really an invitation. Yet she wanted to go. She couldn't explain it, not even to herself. She hadn't been attracted to anyone in a long time and Justin touched something in her. Something that called to her in the most basic way.

And here she was, standing in the lobby of the Carriage House and scanning the room for Justin Beckett.

"Reservation?" the maître d' asked. He smiled admiringly at her.

"Beckett," she said confidently, but Samara didn't know whose name the reservation was in, *if* there was a reservation.

The man looked down a sheet on a podium she

couldn't see over. Then he took a couple large menus and led her to a table in a secluded spot. She couldn't see the door and wouldn't know when Justin arrived until he was practically sliding into the chair opposite her.

"Might I suggest a glass of wine?" he asked, then went on to give her the vintage and year. It matched the date of the vintage photo on the card.

Samara nodded and he offered her the menu, displaying it with exaggerated panache.

Samara smiled, but it had faded by the time the waiter offered her a third glass of wine and Justin had yet to show. Refusing it, she kept looking around, feeling that everyone in the place was staring at her and she somehow had on a sign that said *I'm alone.*

She checked her watch. Asked the waiter for the time and then checked hers again. She'd surveyed her fingernails, twisted her hair, rearranged her silverware and studied the menu more times that she should. Justin was an hour late.

And she was hungry.

Ten minutes later the maître d' came to her table.

"Ms. Scott?" he addressed her by name.

Samara looked up and nodded. "Yes," she said.

"Mr. Beckett has left a message for you. He regrets he's been called away on a family emergency and will not be able to meet you tonight."

"Oh," she said, lost for anything else to say. "Did he say what the emergency was?"

"He didn't give any other details."

"How did you know who I was?" She was sitting alone in a busy restaurant and she'd been here for over an hour. Even she would know who the call was meant for.

"Mr. Beckett described you perfectly. He said to give you anything you want with his compliments." The man nodded slightly in what looked like an almost-bow. "Would you like to order?"

Initially, she thought of refusing. Eating alone wasn't something she planned to do. But she was hungry, and she'd waited for him a considerable amount of time.

"Yes," she told the man. "I would."

Chapter 4

"What do you mean he didn't show up?" Cinnamon Grier stopped in midstride as she and Samara left the National Weather Services office in Virginia. Mac, Cinnamon's husband, stood across the parking lot waiting for them.

"I mean, I sat in the restaurant like a dumb wallflower waiting for him and he never showed up."

Samara had come to Virginia for the weekend. After being stood up, she wanted to get out of the city and it had been a while since she had visited her sister. Mac approached them when they stopped walking.

"What's going on?" he asked.

"Justin stood her up."

"When?" Mac asked.

"Last night. We had a date—"

"A date," Mac said, with a wide smile.

"Not a real date. The man needs to show up to call it a 'date,'" Samara said. "This was the second time I've sat alone in a restaurant because of him."

"The other time he was virtually kidnapped by his ex-wife who might be a little vindictive to you."

"Well, that's her problem, not mine."

"I know, but actually Justin was a victim in that situation, too."

"This time the story I got from the maître d' was he had a family emergency."

"Well, he did," Mac said.

Both women looked at him as if he'd suddenly transformed into a wizard.

"What do you know about it?" Cinnamon asked.

"Justin's sister had a serious accident. He drove home last night."

"Home?" Samara asked. "Where's home?"

"Maryland. He's from Cumberland," Mac said. "It's a couple of hours from here, traffic permitting."

"Is she going to be all right?" Samara asked.

"I haven't heard."

Samara suddenly felt guilty. She'd been angry all night with Justin. Her thoughts of him standing her up had been harsh and unforgiving. Now she discovered he has a valid reason. Family was important to her and she knows she'd drop everything and run to Cinnamon if she were hurt.

"If you want, I can call and find out," Mac offered, reaching for his cell phone.

"Don't do that," Samara stopped him. "I feel like enough of an idiot for thinking the worst of him."

But her brother-in-law didn't take her protest to heart. Right after dinner at the house that used to belong to their grandmother and where Cinnamon and Mac now lived, he told her she had a phone call.

Samara glanced at the place where she'd left her purse. Her cell phone hadn't sounded. And the house phone hadn't rang.

She gave her brother-in-law an askant look.

"You didn't?"

"I was concerned," he said, spreading his hands. "Justin is a good friend and I wanted to be sure he didn't stand up my favorite sister-in-law for nothing."

His smile was infectious. Samara understood why her sister fell for him. But that didn't mean she forgave him for calling Justin. Matchmaking was often attributed to women, but Samara knew that men were just as apt to hook up their friends in relationships, too.

While she had gone out with the thought of it being a date with Justin, they were not in a relationship. She went to the kitchen and picked up the receiver.

Taking a deep breath, she said, "Justin, this is Samara."

"Hello, Samara." His voice sounded surprised, but happy. She could hear his smile through the line. A warm feeling washed over her. She was amazed at how the sound of his voice wiped away her pent-up anger. "I apologize for last night," he began.

"Don't worry about it. It wasn't anything special." She felt her stomach clench at the lie. She'd spent a lot of time getting ready and she felt like a fool sitting alone in that restaurant. But he had a valid reason for not coming. "How's your sister? Mac said she had an accident."

"She was cleaning windows on the second story and fell off a ladder. Her condition is serious, but stable, so we're optimistic," he said, sounding solemn.

"I am so sorry," she said.

"I hate to cut this short, but I'm about to run back to the hospital."

"Oh, I'm sorry. I won't hold you."

"We'll make up that date when I get back."

"We'll talk about it then."

As Samara replaced the receiver, she smiled. It took a moment for her heartbeat to return to normal. She didn't want to return to the living room with the glow of happiness lighting her face and in every move of her body.

Tourists clogged the entry points of most of the monuments in the District from late March or early April, when the Japanese Cherry Blossom Festival began, through December, when the lights of the huge mall Christmas tree were lit by the President. Justin loved the city and didn't mind the tourists. Where he came from in Maryland, there was never this much activity. And the only place that stayed open twenty-four-hours-a-day was an all-night pharmacy.

Justin sat on one of the park benches in Lafayette Park. He watched the rush of families taking pictures of the White House across the street and noted the park police patrolling the area. Of course, there were also plain-clothes Homeland Security people among the crowd, but they were not detectable.

Justin was waiting for Samara. She often walked this way. Like him, the tourists didn't bother her. Seeing her coming, he stood up. She was on the other side of the street, but he knew her walk. Knew the line of her body, the way her hips swayed, the arch of her arms as she swung them easily, the curve of her smile and the brightness of her eyes when she was enjoying herself.

Stepping off the curb, Justin waited for her as she crossed toward the park. There was no traffic in front of the White House. It had been cordoned off years ago as a security measure.

"Samara," he called, not wanting to frighten her by stepping in front of her like a mugger.

She stopped, looking for where the sound had come.

"Here." He raised his hand and jogged a couple of steps.

"Justin," she responded.

Her smile made his heart flip.

"When did you get back?"

"Today." In fact, he'd come here from the airport.

He'd checked in with the office and gone straight to the park where he knew she'd be passing.

"Are things better with your sister?"

He nodded. "She's going to be all right. And thank you for asking."

"That's good. I don't know how I'd survive if something happened to my sister."

"I understand. Deanna and I are very close. In fact, our entire family is close."

"I remember your brother. Do you have a large family?"

Justin fell in step with her. They walked through the park toward Sixteenth Street.

"Three brothers, one sister."

"Five of you. From the same parents?"

"Fortieth anniversary this year."

"That is large. I only have Cinnamon. She's really my half sister, but we never think of each other that way."

"No brothers?"

She shook her head. "None. I envy people with large families. They seem to have so much fun."

"We do," Justin agreed. He smiled, remembering some of the antics that had happened while they were growing up. "There is also the rivalry and sometimes we hate each other. So many personalities, so little room in one house."

"But in the long run, it all works out," she assumed.

He nodded. "The things we did as kids would make my parents' hair stand on end if they knew," he laughed. "I couldn't imagine not having my brothers and sister around."

"Other than Christian, do they all live in Maryland?"

"Only Deanna and Micah live in Maryland. Austin lives in Chicago."

"And you live here. How did you happen to move to D.C.?"

"I went to a job fair while I was still in college. They were recruiting there and I interviewed and got a job."

"I know that's a simplistic answer. People don't work where you do and interview for the job."

"I started in State and moved to other positions."

They stopped for the light at the end of the park. The rush-hour traffic crowded the thoroughfares playing a unique cacophony of sound that happened twice a day. Justin crossed with Samara as the light changed.

Justin didn't want to talk about his job. It wasn't something that he could discuss. He worked for OEO and never knew what he'd be doing from one minute to the next. When word came that Deanna was hospitalized, he had to clear it with his superiors as to whether he would be able to leave. Thankfully, only regular emergencies were the order of the day, nothing dire.

But he was here today and he had to go in, even at this late hour when everyone else was rushing home. It was good he could get off sometimes during regular hours. Like next week when he had plans that involved Samara. And not even world crisis was going to keep him from going through with them.

* * *

The second postcard was sticking out from under the door of her apartment when Samara arrived home. She'd just left Justin, but she knew the card was from him. How he got in the building was a mystery to her, but with his charm he could no doubt talk his way past a simple security guard. After all, he'd charmed his way into her life, despite her objections. She didn't take time to examine those objections. Everyone liked attention and how could a woman resist a man who pursued her with a novel approach.

Inside the screen door was a crystal bud vase with a single white rose in it and a ribbon around the neck. Attached to the ribbon was an envelope. The same block lettering identified her as the intended recipient. Inside she found a single ticket and gasped when she realized what it was for.

Samara picked everything up and went inside. *I apologize for dinner. Let's try it again,* the card read. Again it was a vintage postcard with a photo of the Kennedy Center as it would have looked in the nineteenth century, if it had existed at that time. Samara again experienced that warm feeling that accompanied Justin's gifts. He was having the cards made. She surrendered to emotions that prickled her skin, making her feel good knowing he'd taken the trouble to do something so unique just to go out with her. What other guy would take the time? Justin was different.

Looking at the postcard again, she wondered where

he'd had it made. The Kennedy Center had been built to honor President John F. Kennedy. It opened in 1971. The picture postcard was the same era as the Carriage House restaurant photo had been. Justin had found the right button. The card made her feel so special.

Thank heaven her friends didn't know anything about it. They would tease her to no end. But right now, she didn't care. She was going on a date with Justin Beckett. That shouldn't make her so happy, but it did. It had been a while since a man had paid attention to her. She was a bookish person, someone who liked deciphering old documents. But Justin liked her.

The feeling of joy that warmed her face when she saw the ticket to an August Wilson play stayed with her all the way to the Terrace Theater in the famed Kennedy Center. These tickets were virtually unattainable. This was the play to see and as such, many tickets went to political heavies. Samara had no idea how Justin had garnered them, and she wasn't about to question her good luck.

"Hi," he said, coming up behind her.

Samara whirled around and looked at him. She had to force her mouth from dropping open at the sight of him in a tuxedo. Mainly he wore suits as most of Washington's government executives did, but tonight he was dressed in a tuxedo.

He was gorgeous.

The suit fit him perfectly, from the cut of his broad shoulders to the tapered waist and his long legs. His smile was bright and his dark eyes gleamed as he stared at her. His dark chestnut coloring was emphasized by the whiteness of his shirt.

"Ready?" he asked.

Samara nodded, unable to speak over the lump that lodged in her throat. She hadn't reacted to a man this way in…in never, she thought. She wanted to touch him, feel the fabric of his jacket and the strength of his arms beneath it. In fact, she wanted to run her hands all over him.

Justin took her arm and led her to their seats. Samara took hers and opened her program.

"I hope you haven't already seen this."

"I haven't," she confirmed. "I don't know how you got tickets, but I'm glad you did."

His smile warmed her. Samara had to damp down her internal furnace. She wasn't used to this kind of reaction. If she wasn't careful, Justin would think she was beginning to like him.

And she was.

The lights dimmed and they instinctively looked up, then smiled and gave their attention to the stage. A moment later Justin reached inside his pocket and pulled out an electronic device.

"No," he whispered.

"What's wrong?"

"I hate to do this to you," he said. "But I have to go."

"Go? Why?"

"I can't say but I cannot ignore this message." He

leaned over and kissed her quickly. "I'll make it up to you. I promise."

In a second he was gone, his taste still on her tingling lips.

"I hate men," Samara announced the next night.

"So what's new about that?" Geri asked as she walked along the runway that now stood in the middle of the room where she planned to open the bridal shop.

The place had changed since the group assembled there a couple weeks ago. Instead of a blank room with no fixtures and whitewashed windows, the place now looked like a dress shop. Vinyl dress bags covering wedding gowns hung along one wall. A glass case with white gloves, satin bags and tiaras provided a natural barrier between the entryway and main salon. A dressing room had been meticulously appointed in the back. A dais stood before a wall of mirrors that would give the bride a panoramic view of herself.

"We weren't in the seats more than five minutes before he left me."

"Whom are we talking about?" Carmen asked, coming through the door from the parking lot. She dropped her jacket and purse on a nearby chair.

"Samara had a date."

"Another almost date," Samara corrected. "And I'm finished with men who stand me up."

"You were stood up?" Carmen put her hands on her hips as if it was a personal affront.

"Twice."

"Twice," both women said at once.

"When was the other time?" Diana asked.

Samara hadn't intended to tell them about that. She didn't want to explain everything, but these were her best friends. They would support her in whatever crisis she met.

"A couple weeks ago. He sent me a postcard-invitation to meet him for dinner. He never showed up."

Samara explained that his sister had had a serious accident and she agreed that was a good enough reason to forgive him.

"But this time, at the Center," Shane said, "you were already there and he got up and left?"

"He got a message on one of those electronic umbilical cords that I hate and in seconds it had yanked him out of his seat and was reeling him back to his office." She demonstrated as if she were a mime pulling on a rope.

Samara had a cell phone, but she hated the electronic communication devices that never allowed a person to rest. They were always at work, always checking in, never really leaving the job. Shane and Carmen laughed at her description.

"He *does* work for OEO," Geri reminded them.

"What does that mean?" Shane asked.

"Do you know what goes on there?"

"No," Shane replied. "I don't think anyone does."

"Exactly," Geri said. "But whatever it is, we all agree that it's critical."

"We don't know what it's critical to," Diana said. "We know it's something to do with the government, but the secret is kept close to the breast."

"So anyone working there would have to be in touch at all times. It's like working at the White House."

Which is close enough to be across the street, Samara thought.

"Still," Samara said. "I'm through with him."

"Don't be so hasty," Geri warned.

"And why shouldn't I?"

"Are you kidding?" Geri asked. "In this town where the women outnumber the men a hundred-to-one, you should grab him with both hands."

"A hundred-to-one? Is that all?" Carmen asked. "It feels like five-hundred-to-one to me every Saturday night."

"Whatever it is, a single man with a job is worth at least a good meal," Geri said.

"If you can hold him still long enough to get the salad," Samara said. "And I'm a little busy right now. I can do without someone having me get all dressed up just so I can sit by myself."

"Doing what?" Shane asked. "What are you so busy doing?"

"I have a job. I want to make it a career."

"You want to make yourself so busy that you don't have time for anything else," Geri told her.

"And why you'd want to bury yourself in a vault is beyond me," Shane added, reaching for a bottle of water.

"First of all, it's not a vault," Samara defended. "It's a clean room."

"Same difference," Shane muttered.

"Second, the work is important," Samara went on ignoring the rudeness of her friend. "I get to see the documents that support the structure of this country. In some cases, I even get to touch them."

"Woo-hoo." Carmen curled her finger in the air, mocking the importance of Samara's job.

"Even if you do like making love to all those papers," Geri said, "don't discount actually making love to a man."

"Whose side are you guys on? I thought I could get some support from you."

Geri looked up from fixing the skirt on the runway. "Samara, you do have our support. We just want you to remember that life is for living. And that it's time you lowered that wall around yourself and let someone inside it."

She had, Samara thought. She'd tried to meet Justin for dinner. She'd gone to the Kennedy Center and met him. After spending months telling him she wasn't interested in getting to know him, she'd finally opened the door and look where it led her—to a lonely table in a crowded restaurant and sitting next to the shadow of a ghost in a dark theater.

This was not living.

Chapter 5

Usually Samara slept without a care, but for some reason she was having difficulty tonight. Pushing the covers back, she'd gotten out of bed to get a drink from the kitchen. On the way back, she stopped and turned on the television. Maybe the noise would lull her to sleep.

An hour later, she was still awake. With the two hundred television stations available on her satellite, there was nothing that engaged her. Reaching for the remote and switching it off, she got up. The ringing of the telephone startled her and she jumped. It was the house phone.

The pre-World War II building still operated a

twenty-four-hour security desk instead of installing an intercom system. It was the old world style that had appealed to Samara when she'd looked at the place.

"Ms. Scott," the night clerk said. "You have a guest asking to come up."

She understood the code. A "guest" was male and a "visitor" was female.

"Who is it?" she asked.

"Mr. Justin Beckett."

"Beckett," she said out loud, not intending to. His was the last name she expected to hear. At this time of night, if anyone dropped by unannounced it would be one of her best friends.

"Shall I let him up?" the clerk asked.

Indecision made her hesitate a moment.

"Ms. Scott?"

"Yes," she said. Then she looked at her nightgown. Rushing to the bedroom, she grabbed the first thing her hand touched, a full-length skirt and pushed her legs into it. She'd zipped it up and pulled a sleeveless shirt over her head. The doorbell was ringing before she had time to pull a brush through her hair or apply lipstick.

Grabbing a lip gloss from the dresser, she ringed her mouth with the clear gel and pushed the tube into her pocket as she pulled the door open.

"Are you speaking to me?" Justin asked. His smile was charming, but there was a tired look about his eyes.

"I shouldn't be," she said, stepping back and allowing him access to the apartment.

Justin looked around and nodded. "I expected antiques."

"Carmen likes antiques. I'm strictly contemporary." Her apartment had calm gray walls that were offset with mahogany crown molding and baseboards. The furniture picked up the color scheme and added various shades of violet and pink. The throw pillows were bold colors and her tables were also of the same mahogany as the woodwork.

"I saw your light and thought I'd try to explain what happened."

"That would be interesting to hear." Samara led him to the sofa. "Would you like something to drink? Or eat? You look like you haven't been home in a while." His suit was disheveled. Samara pictured him as she'd seen him in the lobby of the Kennedy Center. While he still had on a suit and tie, this was Justin the working man. The other one was a lover.

"I ate something at lunch, but don't ask me what it was. I've been home once since leaving you at the Kennedy Center."

"What's going on?" she asked, going to the kitchen and pouring him a large glass of orange juice. "Drink this. It's better than coffee."

Returning to the kitchen, she checked to see what she could prepare with as little effort as possible. Justin appeared in the doorway. Immediately her senses when into overdrive. What was it? she thought. Why did she react to him this way?

"How about breakfast?" she asked.

He checked his watch. "I suppose it is that time." He saw Samara as she glanced at the clock over the sink. "Can I help with anything?"

"Apartment kitchens aren't made for two people. Why don't you sit down and tell me what's going on?"

Samara laid bacon strips on a microwavable plate and set it in the microwave.

"There isn't much I can say, but let me start by apologizing again for having to leave the play."

"I was angry," she admitted. "Especially when it was the second time." Getting eggs, she broke several in a bowl and whisked them into a froth.

"It's the job," Justin said. "When the phone rings, I fly."

"And why are you free tonight?"

"I wasn't. I just left the office."

"At this hour?"

"There are no clocks in my office. We operate on an emergency basis and everything is an emergency."

He sounded tired. Samara's heart went out to him. She wanted to go to him and put her arms around him, but she continued with the food preparation.

"I know I shouldn't ask, but I'm going to," she told him. "What do you do there?"

He stared at her, but said nothing. Samara knew she wasn't going to get an answer.

"Should I be concerned?" Turning the eggs into an omelet pan, Samara continued her choreograph of making a meal.

"I'm not sure. We haven't defined our relationship."

"Do you like what you do?" Samara changed the subject immediately. She wasn't going to discuss a relationship. Dinner and a play didn't constitute a relationship. She was done with those.

Taking two plates from the cabinet, she filled them with food and set them on the table. "More juice?" she asked, holding the container. He nodded and she refilled his glass.

They sat down and he dug into the food. For a few moments they ate in silence. Samara watched him wondering what had kept him so busy that he hadn't eaten.

"Thank you for being so nice," he said, pushing his empty plate aside.

She thought he meant the food until he continued.

"Most women wouldn't have let me get past the desk clerk."

"You can thank Geri for that."

"Geri?"

"My friend. She owns Shadow Walk. She said I should give you another chance."

He smiled, the dimple in his left cheek catching her eye. The tiredness left his face for a moment. "I'll have to thank her when we meet."

"You should have gone home and gotten some sleep," Samara said as if he knew her feelings.

"And miss spending a few moments with you?" He shook his head from side to side. "No way."

Instantly, Samara felt as if she were standing in front

of an open flame. One that flash-burned only to ignite an internal furnace. Her throat went dry and she searched for some kind of coherent response, but nothing came to mind. She reached for her own glass of juice. She had to force the liquid down her throat, but it helped to release her tongue from the dry glue that kept it still.

For a long moment they stared at each other as if suspended in time. Samara wasn't sure if everything in the universe had ceased moving. Justin held her gaze. Images, unbidden, flew through her mind of the two of them standing in her doorway, of his mouth on hers, of him kissing her quickly before leaving her seated at the Kennedy Center.

She wanted him to kiss her again, to hold her, make her his. And as if reading her mind, Justin obliged. He stood up and reached for her hand. She stared at his hand for a moment before placing hers in it. With only a tug, he pulled her out of her chair and in one fluid movement she was in his arms.

Her face was close to his. She breathed in the scent of him. Even long days and nights confined in his work didn't remove the unique fragrance that attacked her senses and had her reeling toward him.

"I've been thinking about this for days," he said.

"About what?" Samara hedged, although she, too, was dreaming of him, angry at the loss of anticipation for just this moment.

"Let me show you." His mouth dropped onto hers.

Arms, with the strength of steel bands, circled her waist and pulled her into the rock-solid wall of his body. Samara groaned as spasms of need and pleasure rocketed through her. Justin's tongue ventured deeply into her mouth and she welcomed his invasion. Her arms found their way around his neck. Going up on tiptoes, her head lolled back as Justin deepened the kiss.

Never had Samara felt like this, as if the ground was no longer beneath her feet, as if she were floating, dancing in the middle of a room with no ceiling and no floor. Samara's hands roamed over his shoulders and arms. She wanted to be closer, feel his skin, relish in the luster of fire and ice, heat and cold, silk and wool.

In moments she was tearing at his shirt, pulling it free and running her fingers under the expensive fabric. Justin's hands curled at the hem of her shirt and ran upward to her breasts. As they found her nipples and teased them into a taut life, she shuddered with delight.

"This is crazy," she muttered to herself.

"I know," Justin answered. "But it's a phenomenal kind of crazy."

Phenomenal wasn't the word for it, Samara thought. There was no word to describe how she was feeling, how Justin was making her feel, drawing out emotions she thought were dead or asleep. He'd awakened them and they were screaming for fulfillment.

Samara pulled her mouth free. Air rushed into her lungs like she'd opened a vacuum. She didn't want to release the claim he had on her movements, but the need to breathe forced her to break from him. His mouth was hot and seeking and she wanted nothing more than to allow the pleasurable assault to continue.

"Come," she whispered. Taking his hand, she led him to the bedroom. The covers on the bed were rumpled where she'd been sleeping, but the other side was as untouched as it had been when she made it that morning.

But things had changed.

Justin turned her into his arms and found her mouth. All thought left Samara's mind except the delicious syrup that flowed over her at his touch.

"I hope you have a condom," she said against his mouth.

"Never leave home without it," he teased.

He pulled her shirt over her head and tossed it high in the air. Samara took only a moment to watch it floating upward. Her hands were busy with the buttons on his shirt. In moments they were undressed and reaching for each other. Justin's hands smoothed down her back and over her hips. Samara shuddered as tiny firecrackers exploded under her skin. Arching her back and pressing herself closer to him, she felt every inch of his dark skin. And it made her aggressive, brazen even.

She wrapped her right leg around his left one and shimmied up and down his body. Lightning sparked between them like a live wire snapping in the rain. Samara kissed his shoulders and proceeded across his chest. She felt his breathing accelerate, heard the thump of his heart as it boomed against her mouth. Big hands cupped her buttocks and pushed her against his erection. Her head fell back and she cried out as erotic sensations racked her.

Justin lowered her to the bed. His mouth kissed her lips, her chin, her cheeks. His hands massaged her sides and skimmed over her breasts which sat at attention waiting for his discovery. Time seemed to speed up as they traded touch for touch, kiss for kiss, caress for caress.

As suddenly as a dam breaking, their need exploded. They fought for dominance, each desperate in pursuit of the other. Justin's mouth was wild on hers. Hunger, that of a starving man, pressed her into the mattress. With lightning speed, Justin retrieved the condom and protected them.

Before she had time to feel the coolness of the air between them, he was with her. He looked down at her, skimming her features as his eyes traveled over her. She felt no shame. No nakedness. She wanted him to look, wanted him to touch her with his eyes, to feel his hands forming her skeleton, covering her muscles and planing her skin.

Inside her anticipation built until she thought she'd burst. Justin must have understood. Moving his legs over hers, he entered her. She thought she was prepared for the entry-rapture, for that shocking burst of pleasure their joining produced. But the burst was a crescendo, a powerful drug that surged through her as if it had been gathered from past ages and delivered full force at this one moment.

Her legs locked around his hips, capturing him in her own personal prison. Together they danced the primal dance of life, of love, of a need so strong it created worlds. Samara was incapable of holding anything back. Her body was totally involved and totally his for the taking. She thrust it upon him, giving what he gave, taking what she wanted, abandoning anything except the insatiable need that pushed her onward, the raw power of her body's desire.

Inside her rolled timeless waves, shattering vortices, cataclysmic volcanoes changed her, reformed her into another being until, with a final cry, she crashed back to the present.

Her breath was strangled, harsh, mingling with Justin's as they both forced oxygen into lungs that craved it. The room spun for Samara. She could discern nothing. They'd been carried somewhere else, created another setting that was theirs alone. Slowly the spinning returned her to surroundings she recognized.

She still carried Justin's weight. Like a heavy blanket, he covered her, keeping her warm and connected to him in the most intimate way. Running her hands over his back, she found him warm and moist with the dew of sex. The room snapped with the aftermath of their coming.

"That was fantastic," he said, sliding to her side and pulling her against him as if he didn't want to separate yet. Samara didn't.

"It was," she agreed. His lovemaking was like none she'd experienced in the past. She wasn't sure she'd ever find another to equal him.

Running his hand over her face, he pushed her hair back and smiled at her in the semidarkness.

"You're beautiful," he said. His voice was thick with emotion. "I knew you would be."

His eyes closed then and he slept. Samara watched him. He was beautiful, too. More than she ever thought possible. He had held her like a doll that could break, then made love to her as if he never wanted to stop.

She brushed his face with her hand, feeling the five-o'clock stubble on his chin. She kissed his lips, cradled him to her and let the sensations that racked through her have free rein.

The Washington of yesterday is not the Washington of today. Justin got out of his car whistling. No day could be more perfect than this one. And tomorrow had all the earmarks of being perfect, too.

The night he'd spent in Samara's arms, the love they had made, was beyond anything he'd experienced before—or could even hope for.

Mac Grier waved at him as he reached the street.

"What are you doing here?" Justin asked.

"An early interview on the Hill. I thought I'd walk," Mac answered.

"Anything interesting going on?" Justin asked. Mac

was an anchor on the news. His crew would already be setting up and whomever he was interviewing had to be important.

"Nothing out of the ordinary."

Justin knew "ordinary" in Washington was never ordinary. He had his own position at OEO to tell him that. He dealt with emergencies that were international incidents in the making. Occasionally he had to intervene when Americans acted stupidly in overseas situations by buying or selling drugs and getting caught. Mostly, he was involved with the political arena, keeping the cold war *cold.* Most people thought the war ended with the fall of the Soviet Union, but all it did was trade one set of problems for another.

Still, this morning, Justin whistled.

"You're in a good mood," Mac said.

"It's a great day," Justin remarked. Forget that it was hot and humid and promised to be worse as the sun rose higher in the sky. Justin was too happy to care.

"Finally get lucky?" Mac teased.

"I do not kiss and tell."

"You *did* get lucky."

It had to be written on his face. There was no way of concealing it from the world. He was in love and he didn't care who knew.

"Well, at least tell me her name. Is it my sister-in-law?"

Justin said nothing. For the time being he wanted to remain inside a fantasy world, one that he and Samara occupied.

"Maybe I should have Cinnamon invite the two of you down for the weekend."

"Your interview must be waiting," Justin said. With a handshake, he turned onto Seventeenth Street and started whistling again.

Samara punched the power button on the CD player at the same time she kicked her heels off from a day at work. She felt like dancing. Tina Turner's rendition of *Private Dancer* started to play. All day long Samara had thought of Justin and their night together. Nothing else could hold her attention and several times she'd had to be asked questions twice.

She sang along with Tina and danced about the room in her stocking feet. She wondered if this was how her sister felt when she was falling in love with her husband?

Samara stopped. Falling in *love? Husband?*

That wasn't it, she told herself. It's just been a while since she had the attentions of a man. She switched off the CD player, no longer interested in the song or the dance.

While she liked Justin, enjoyed his company and the way he made her feel, she was not falling for him. And marriage! What was she thinking? She knew that was not for her.

Chapter 6

"This is a surprise," Diana said as Samara entered her office. "What gets you up here?"

Diana's office was on the top floor of one of the many office buildings in the Crystal City complex across the Potomac in Virginia.

"I was in the neighborhood."

"Sure you were," Diana countered. "The Archives is right around the corner."

"Well, I wasn't in the neighborhood, but I'm here now."

"I'm about done here. Why don't we go somewhere and eat and talk?"

Diana's desk was cluttered with storyboards and papers. In the corners sat large mock-ups of ads for lipstick, toothpaste, designer gowns. Her phone constantly rang and she was directing an entire orchestra of details.

"Are you sure?"

Diana nodded. "It never ends. It'll be here tomorrow."

Diana got up and slipped her arms into the white suit jacket that hung on the back of her chair. Not far from her office was a score of different restaurants, each with different ethnicities and different types of food. Diana had often stated that New York only thought it had the United Nations. Virginia really had it. They settled on Thai food and were seated at low tables among a color scheme of red and black.

Diana waited until the waiter brought their food before asking, "What is it?"

"What?"

"The real reason you happened to be in the neighborhood."

Samara took a drink of the wine they'd ordered. "I wanted to talk to you."

"About what?"

"Greg."

"My Greg?"

Samara nodded. Diana had met her fiancé, Gregory McKnight, two years ago at a party. Greg was an economist and worked for the Treasury Department.

"What do you want to know?"

"Are you sure he's the one?" Samara asked.

"Absolutely," Diana said without hesitation.

"The statistics aren't with you," Samara argued.

"Statistics? I'm not going to run my life by statistics. Honestly, Samara, you've been cooped up in that dungeon way too long."

The "dungeon" was what Diana called the subbasement workrooms where the rare documents were stored and restored.

"What's happened? I know you like Greg and that you're not against me marrying him. So what has caused you to think about statistics and whether he's the right one? Who is your *he?*"

Samara took a deep breath. "I don't have a *he.* I've just been wondering lately. A lot of my friends are married or getting married." She paused and looked at the huge rock on Diana's left hand. "And since Cinnamon also took the plunge, I find myself wondering…"

"What happened to 'a lot of my friends are divorced'?" she mocked. "The statistics thing? The I'll-never…" Diana suddenly stopped. "It's Justin. What happened?"

Samara put her hands up. "Diana, don't jump the gun."

"You're falling for him," she stated.

"I am not."

"What happened the other night? The August Wilson play?"

"I got to the Kennedy Center and Justin met me. But as soon as we got to our seats, he got a call and he was gone."

"Again!"

She nodded. "But he came by last night."

"And something happened." Again it was a statement.

"More than something."

"So, you are falling for him?"

Samara thought about it. The question had been at the back of her mind since she woke up in his arms. It wasn't a "morning after" she wanted. She wanted him around longer. But she wasn't sure that was possible. He'd already proven unreliable more than once. Should she forget about a relationship before it got started?

"I think I am," Samara finally said.

Samara was sure the housework gene was missing from her set of forty-six chromosomes, but no one seeing her cleaning her apartment would believe that. She'd totally redone the bedroom, even to the point of moving some of the furniture around. Justin had been in that room. His imprint was there. She needed to make it different, remove him from the surroundings.

It was strange, Samara thought as she scrubbed the kitchen cabinets with oil soap, that this much effort was necessary for a man she hadn't known for more than a few months. They'd met a couple of years ago, but she really didn't know him, had consciously avoided getting to know him. And now she felt the need to work him out of her life.

By five in the afternoon she was done, exhausted and grimy. And she was angry.

Why hadn't he called? They'd spent the night together, awakened in each other's arms. He'd said he would call. She remembered the two of them entwined in each other's arms and heat swept through her like a wildfire. She had to get him out of her thoughts and out of her life. She would call and tell him not to come, that she wasn't interested in a relationship.

She lifted the phone and punched in his number, but replaced the receiver before it rang. She wouldn't do it on the phone. It was cowardly. She needed to face him and tell him this was not a road she wished to travel. It was better that way, for both of them, better to not get involved.

Throwing herself back into cleaning, she dusted and polished all the tables. When she finished, the phone did ring. Her heart lurched. Forcing herself not to rush, she walked quickly to the phone and answered. She tried not to sound disappointed when she heard Diana's voice with her fiancé talking in the background.

"What are you doing?" Diana asked.

"Cleaning, why?"

"I want to see the gown," Diana said.

"What?"

"The one you found in the trunk. Carmen says it's beautiful. So I thought I'd like to see it in case I want one that resembles it or want to take it off your hands. If not, maybe Geri can use it in the fashion show. Mind if I come look?"

"Come on over."

"See you in a bit." She hung up.

Samara looked at the clock. It was after five o'clock and Justin still hadn't called.

Samara was glad she was ending her relationship with Justin anyway.

Going to the bathroom, she turned on the shower. Maybe he was called to work again, she rationalized as she stepped under the spray.

Samara grabbed the shampoo and poured a liberal amount over her hair. She scrubbed it into each strand, lathering it into a froth, then scrubbing her scalp with her fingers. She didn't know how long she did that before allowing the water to rinse away the suds.

Wrapped in a large towel, she left the bathroom. The trunk with the wedding gown sat against the wall. Samara hesitated only a moment before going to it and lifting the lid. The dress waited like a sentinel. She picked it up and stared at it. Then, impulsively, she took it to the bedroom, threw it on the bed and searched for suitable underwear. When clothed, she stepped into the dress.

Lightning didn't strike.

But when she turned around and stared in the mirror, her mouth dropped open. The dress was beautiful and it made her look beautiful, too. She admired herself, turning one way and then the other. She buttoned all the buttons and looked at her back again. And at that moment the house phone rang.

"Your guest is here," the clerk said.

"Send them up," she said.

Diana had brought Greg with her. Didn't she know it was bad luck for the groom to see the bride in her gown. Well, *Diana* wouldn't be *in* the gown. And Greg could always wait in the living room. Samara rushed to the door when the bell rang. Yanking it open, her arms spread to model the gown, she froze in place when she recognized Justin standing there, a bouquet of flowers in his hand and an expression on his face that went from surprise to incredulity.

She wanted to slam the door closed, but she was unable to move.

"I— Justin…" She could think of nothing to say. "I wasn't expecting you."

"I see," he said, looking her up and down.

"I mean…you didn't call."

"I know. I got tied up at work."

Samara felt relieved. For an awkward moment they stood there.

"These are for you." He thrust the flowers at her. "I'll leave."

"No," she said too quickly to her own ears. "Come on in."

He walked in cautiously.

"This is the dress that was in the trunk." She turned for his approval.

"A wedding gown. Well, you look gorgeous," he said, staring at her and shaking his head. Even though the gesture was negative, the communication was totally positive. He walked around her, taking in all details of the gown. "Why are you wearing it? You aren't getting married, are you?"

She laughed, nervously. "I have a friend who's engaged. She wanted to see the dress and impulsively I put it on."

"She can't look as beautiful in it as you do."

Again Samara's body was suffused with heat. "Stay here, I'll take it off."

"I could help," he said.

The air between them turned electric. Samara forgot everything she'd thought of saying. Justin took a step toward her. Just as his arms reached for her, the phone rang a second time.

Diana gasped when Samara opened the door. "You're *wearing* the dress?" Her hand went to her mouth and she took a step back as if some evil spell would touch her.

Samara looked down. Since Justin arrived, she'd been thrown into confusion.

"I thought you said it was bad luck," Diana said. She came into the apartment, walking straight into the living room, then stopped when Justin stood up.

"Hello," she said. "I didn't know Samara had company."

"This is Justin Beckett," Samara introduced. "Justin, my friend Diana Quade. She's the one getting married."

"And Samara is apparently my model." Diana glanced at Samara.

Diana shook hands with Justin. Samara was relieved when Diana didn't make a fuss over meeting him.

"Congratulations," Justin said.

"Thank you." Diana smiled and blushed.

"Where's Greg? I thought he was with you," Samara asked.

"He's in the lobby. He said he shouldn't see the gown. And if he waited, I wouldn't stay long."

Samara smiled, acknowledging Greg's technique for keeping Diana on time. She often got caught up in whatever she was doing, and clocks didn't seem to exist in her world. Samara was sure that it would be up to the bridesmaids to make sure she got to the ceremony on time.

"We're on our way to dinner. Why don't you two join us?" Diana looked from Samara to Justin and back.

"We'd love to," Justin answered her. "I've been trying to buy her a meal for months."

Diana turned and winked at Samara. "She does look a little on the thin side. Maybe that's how she got into that dress. I can see it's way too small for me."

"Diana, the dress can be altered if you like it. Personally, I don't think it's your style."

Diana agreed with her. "But on you, it looks fantastic. Turn around." Diana used her hand to make a circle.

Samara twirled in the gown. The bottom ballooned out and the train fell into perfect folds.

"What do you think, Justin?" Diana asked.

"I think it's perfect."

"You know Samara is never going to marry."

"Diana!" Samara warned. "Justin isn't interested…"

"She says that marriage only ends in divorce, so why bother. It just messes up two people's lives, if you're lucky."

"Let me guess," Justin said. "Divorced parents?"

"No," Samara answered. "Just about everyone else I know."

"Including me," Justin added.

"Well, you *are* divorced," Samara countered.

"But I'm not down on the entire practice."

"Neither am I. It's just not for me."

She didn't want to discuss this now and wanted to throttle Diana for bringing up the subject.

"I'm going to change now. Diana, get Justin something to drink while I put something else on."

"Sure."

Samara went toward her bedroom as Diana hummed the *Wedding March.*

"Diana sure has marriage on her brain," Justin commented after dinner and waving good-night to Greg and Diana. "By all the comments on falling in love and getting married. Only I had the feeling she wasn't talking about herself."

"She wasn't," Samara admitted. "They were messages for me, thinly veiled, but I understood them."

"What do they mean?"

"You already know this," Samara told Justin. "I've already outlined my beliefs to you."

"About never getting married."

She tossed her head. "I have no desire and no need to marry. I can support myself and I don't need or believe I need anyone else to fulfill my life."

"And the probability of divorce is high."

"That, too."

"Samara, that is such a defeatist attitude. People fall in love and marry every day."

Justin started the car and pulled out of the parking lot. The lights of the District reflected off the various museums and monuments.

"I'm simply not going to fall in love," she told him.

"You have no control over that."

"You mean, your chemistry theory?" she asked.

"Somewhat, but not totally. Chemistry only gives you biology. Love is what bonds two people together. And unless you imprison yourself in a tower on some deserted island, you can't stop love from finding you."

"Your attitude is rather strange," Samara argued. "You were married. You loved your wife when you took your vows, didn't you?"

He nodded.

"Look what happened to that."

"But at least we tried. You're deciding not to try something because of statistics. Why did you go for your job at the Archives? The odds of you not getting it had to be pretty high. Yet you beat them."

"You can't compare a job to marriage," she dismissed.

"Why not? Both of them require work—a lot of work. Hard work. And it's got to be done every day. But if the two people are right for each other, it's worth it."

Samara thought of her sister, Cinnamon, and Mac. They were perfect for each other. Samara's parents had gone through some rocky times. They were still married, but Samara wasn't sure they were the best match. Her dad had once been married to Cinnamon's mother. No two people were ever so mismatched as her sister's mother and her own father, but in the back of Samara's mind, she believed they each were the love of the other's life.

How could she put herself through something like that? How was it possible to know the right man? Find him? Out of all the people in the universe, how was it possible to settle on one man you could love, respect and spend your life with? The statistics told her. It was too impossible to know.

"Why did you put that dress on today?" Justin interrupted her thoughts.

"What?"

"Why did you put on a wedding gown today?"

"I—I was cleaning when Diana called and said she wanted to see the gown, so I took it out of the trunk. I just put it on. There was no other motive."

"No?" He raised his eyebrows.

At P Street he turned left, the opposite direction from her apartment.

"You admit the gown is beautiful?" he asked.

"Yes," she agreed, refusing to let him know she thought the dress was gorgeous and Samara felt wonderful wearing it.

"Did you feel like a bride?"

"What? Why this third degree over a dress?"

"Because it isn't just a dress. It represents a marriage,

a combining of two lives, two families, the wedding of two people who love each other. And you wanted to feel those things when you put it on."

"So every model who walks down a runway wearing a wedding gown is secretly yearning for home and hearth?"

"You weren't a model. Models wear clothes as a profession. That was not what you were doing today."

"I could have been. Just for your information, Geri is opening a bridal shop and she's asked me to model in a fashion show to mark the store's premiere."

"And you're going to model that dress?"

"Can we drop this? I feel like I'm on some witness stand, explaining something that needs no explanation."

"All right," he said.

Samara looked out the window. They were on Wisconsin Avenue near the Cathedral.

"Where are we going?" she asked.

"Nowhere," he said. "We're here."

He parked the car in front of a large house on a side street that was lined with trees. Getting out, he came around and opened the door for her.

"Where is *here?*"

"This is where I live. I thought you'd like to see it."

"What's your ulterior motive?" she asked, standing on the pavement.

"Turnabout is fair play."

"I don't understand."

His hand went to the small of her back and, giving her a slight push, he led her up the walkway.

"When I think of you, I can imagine you in a specific place. When you think of me, you have no boundaries, no space that reflects who I am or how I live. This is it."

He opened the front door and they stepped inside a large foyer.

"You assume that I think of you," she said.

"It's more than an assumption." He kicked the door closed and turned her into his arms.

"Tell me I'm wrong."

Chapter 7

Justin watch Samara open her mouth to speak, but nothing came out. His eyes locked with hers. Desire flared within him, hot and hungry. She'd been on his mind since he left her in her bedroom a day and a half ago. He'd spent most of that time at the office, but she was never more than a microsecond from his consciousness.

And now she was in his arms. In his home.

"Isn't it unusual for a single man to live in a house?" she asked. "District living is apartment living."

"If you're asking if I lived here with my ex-wife, the answer is no. We lived in Maryland. After the divorce, I bought this place. It was closer to work and I'd become used to living in a house."

"Show me around," she said. "I am supposed to be able to picture you in a specific place, right?"

Justin walked her through the living room, dining room and kitchen. He showed her the great room and a small home office.

"There are three bedrooms upstairs," he said. He didn't take her there because he knew where that would lead.

They returned to the great room. She sat on the sofa in front of the huge fireplace. "Would you like something to drink? Juice, coffee, wine, anything?"

"Trying to get me drunk?"

"It was an innocent question, Samara."

"Wine," she said, with apology in her voice. "White."

He poured them each a glass and handed her one. Sitting down next to her, he said, "I like your friends, Diana and Greg. They make a good couple."

Samara nodded. "I've known Diana since I moved to the District. She met Greg about two years ago. They've been inseparable since."

"That was about the same time we met."

She nodded slowly. He knew she understood the inference.

"Justin, I think you should take me home now."

Her comment was almost an assault. He hadn't expected her to say that. "Why?"

"Obviously, there isn't going to be a you and me. I think you should drop me and find someone more suitable to focus your attention on."

"Why don't you think that person is you?"

"I don't want it to be," she said.

He was amazed the air was still going in and out of his lungs. She intrigued him more than any woman ever had and that included his ex-wife. He'd never known anyone so sure of herself, even if he felt her assurance was misplaced.

"I have a hard time believing that," he said.

"Why?"

"A couple of nights ago, when we were rolling around on the sheets, I would have bet money *that* was more the truth than your words."

Her skin was light enough for him to see the color inch into her face.

"You'd be wrong," she said.

"Really?" he asked.

She stared at him steadily, no thought of wavering that he could see.

"Really."

"That sounds like a challenge."

"It wasn't."

He set his glass on the coffee table. Then reached for hers. She resisted slightly, then let go of the glass. Placing it next to his, he turned back to her.

"Say that again."

Samara didn't say anything. He stared at her, his body aroused. She had no idea how much she affected him. Thoughts of her could produce physical awareness. With her present, within reach, he was apt to spontaneously combust.

Justin moved closer. His mouth nearly touched hers. His arms went around her waist and he pulled her into his arms. She came without resistance. Dressed in a soft white blouse and dark skirt she'd had on at dinner, Justin caressed her. He liked the feel of the fabric. It was as soft as the skin it covered. His hands skimmed over it, over her. His eyes surveyed her features. Her face was close enough for him to savor the perfection nature had given her.

He wanted Samara. He was in no doubt of that. He wanted to touch her all over. Sitting on the sofa was too confining. Justin stood up, pulling Samara her to her feet, too. His mouth took hers, and he kissed her hard. He wanted to devour her, to make her his. Too blot from her mind all the misconceptions and beliefs that there was no future for them.

His hands roved freely, up and down her back, into her hair, angling her mouth to his as if they were seared together.

"I think it's time you saw the bedroom," he whispered against her lips.

"Is this part of the challenge?"

"Definitely," he answered.

Unlike her apartment, where the bedroom was only a door away, his was upstairs. He needed her now, wanted her in his bed. The bedroom was a floor away, almost at the other end of the house. He didn't know if he could make it, didn't know if the force that both pulled them together and kept them in individual bodies would allow him to get that far. Reluctant to let her go,

Justin slipped his arms around her and together they crossed to the stairs. His mouth crushed hers as they slowly mounted each step.

It was almost a dance, them turning and swirling, kissing and releasing, as they moved up one step at time. Their hands touched, fondled. Heads bobbed, teeth clashed, bodies meshed.

Samara felt good in his arms. He couldn't get her out of his thoughts. He wondered, why her? Why did he keep coming back to her when she'd asked him to go? It could be the challenge. He could rarely resist a challenge, but he wouldn't keep coming back if there wasn't something in it he wanted. Why did his arms know the exact circle of her waist, his hands the curvature of her arms, the moon-shape of her buttocks? But it was his mind that she held prisoner. She'd seeped into his brain, into the minute crevices of his being and taken up residence. And he didn't want a change of address. He wanted her to want the same.

Inside the bedroom door, Justin allowed space between them. With his back against the door, he traced the neckline of her blouse. His fingers, brushing against her skin, was the only contact their bodies made. Fire danced through his hands, but for the moment he only looked at her, drank in her features. She stared back.

Moonlight streaked across this part of the room, cutting a path over her eyes and leaving the remainder of her face in semidarkness. Desire lurked in their depths.

Justin ran his hand down her cheek. Slowly he bent

toward her. Her features blurred as he moved closer and closer. His mouth touched hers. They melted into each other. Need grew until he was bending her backward and fighting to control his desire to push her to the floor and take her there.

She pushed him away, taking several steps back until there was space enough for him to see her entire body. With unhurried movements, Justin watched as Samara crossed her arms, gathering the hem of her blouse and pulled it over her head. Her hair, pulled upward with the blouse, spilled back to her shoulders as if in slow motion, the action played back frame by frame. Her hands moved to the zipper on her skirt and guided it downward until it reached the end. Pushing the skirt down, it fell to the floor in a silent heap.

Stepping out if it, she walked toward him. He watched her hips sway from side to side, her body tight and hard, his mind bewitched as it focused on every nuance of her movement, himself a camera and she the principal subject of his mental movie.

Pushing away from the door and moving to meet her, he undid the buttons on his shirt and left it behind him. Her hands met his and together they released his belt. His mouth took hers again with the same desperation as that of a starving man.

Her skin was hot and moist where his hands touched. He caught one of her legs and raised it to his waist. Then the other joined it until her held her, wrapped to him. He walked to the bed, holding her. She slid down his body, forcing a groan from his throat as her hips collided with his erection.

In a flash he removed the rest of his clothes and covered himself with a condom. He kissed her neck and worked his way down her body, removing any vestige of clothing she was still wearing. They fell onto the bed.

Justin wrapped himself around her, drawing her to him, pulling her inward as if he needed her to be part of his makeup, part of him, inside the same skin, sharing the same heartbeat.

He heard her sounds, listened to the rapid beating of her heart, felt her taut, swollen nipples that seemed perfect for his mouth. Unable to wait any longer, he entered her. Her body sheathed him, strong muscles tightening and holding him before relaxing and beginning the routine again.

The rhythm began like drum beats, not in his head, but in his entire being. Faster and faster they sounded, pushing him into her, as if his life depended on it.

Samara met him with a force he'd never known. His tongue dipped deeply into her mouth, plunging, mating, dancing, fighting, dominating. Sounds smacked as their heads moved, shifted, their lips seeking each other's. Justin's arms welded her to him. She was soft, like cotton candy, a pure confection that could evaporate on touch, but she remained solid in his arms.

In a moment, she pushed him over, reversing positions. He pulled her closer, his body going to heaven at the way her hips pumped into him. Justin ran his hands down her body, starting with the area right above her breasts. He felt her pounding heartbeat, and heard the hitch in her throat when his fingers encountered her puckered nipples. Stopping at her waist, he held on to her, riding the curve of her hips until he was sure they would explode.

"Sam," he groaned.

He lifted her, joining her in the pace she set, matching her movements as she took from him what he had to give. He filled her, rooted himself inside her. The sound that came from her throat was music to him. He drove harder, holding her in place, feeling the softness of her flesh as his hands contracted and relaxed in the same rhythm as he plunged and released inside her. He couldn't get enough of her. She clung to him, holding on as she rode him, rode hard and fast, harder and faster, so fast he thought he'd break through the bed.

But it felt good. She felt good. He was lost. Out of control. Unable and unwilling to stop. He was going to die here, the two of them in a rapid fireball that ignited and consumed them. Yet the prospect of it did nothing to quail his energy. If anything he pumped faster and harder into her.

He felt her scream. Justin had never shouted before. He thought it was Samara shouting, but the voice when it registered in his ears was his own. He was calling her name over and over and over. "Sam…Sam…Sam."

Sweat poured from them both. She collapsed against

him, her slick, liquid body spent. Gasping and gulping air, he knew he was in trouble.

Samara Scott may spout the words of an ice princess. She may look cool and in control on the floor of the Archives building. She might present that face to her colleagues and friends, but to him she was fire, hot, blistering, consuming, electrifying, passionately torrid.

And she brought out the beast in him.

The moon was full when Samara opened her eyes. She wasn't disoriented at finding herself in a strange bed, in a strange house, with a man who was anything but a stranger. She smiled, stretching against Justin like a cat waking after a satisfying nap.

Justin was warm to the touch. She ran her hands over his arms and shoulders and fit her frame into his. He slept soundly, without snoring. Samara's stomach growled. She was hungry. *This* time for food. While she'd eaten at dinner, that was hours ago.

Slipping out of bed, she grabbed Justin's shirt and pulled it over her head. Pushing the sleeves up to her elbows, she glanced at him. Blowing a kiss, she went to the kitchen in search of food.

"When does this man eat?" she questioned. "What does he eat?" The refrigerator had nothing in it but orange juice, eggs, bottled water and a bottle of Dom Perignon. Eggs and champagne.

She decided to scramble some eggs and seeing a

blender on the counter, make her version of an Orange Julius drink. She poured the juice in it, added an egg, found some sugar and ice and blended them into a slush. The scrambled eggs finished her impromptu meal.

It didn't take long to eat, but it did satisfy her hunger. Samara took her glass of juice and walked through other rooms. Justin had given her a tour, but she wanted to see more of the space where he lived. He'd said she could imagine him in a specific place. She wanted to ground him in her memory.

The great room was where they had started. She walked through the dining room, which had contemporary furniture, complete with bone china in the cabinet. The table and chairs were dust-free. Samara wondered if he had a cleaning service.

In the office stood the standard desk, laptop computer and cabinet all in a dark cherrywood that made it look rich. The space however, was free of clutter.

Returning to the great room, she walked about the room, looking at the only photo in the room. It sat on a bookcase. She assumed it was of his family. The three men and one woman all resembled each other. Replacing the photo to its original location, she curled up on the sofa with her glass of juice and enjoyed the quiet.

"Hi." Justin came up behind her. "I missed you." He took the glass of juice and drank half of the remaining amount.

"I was hungry. I cooked the food you had available."

Coming around, he dropped into the seat next to her,

wearing only a pair of jeans. "Sorry, I don't eat here much. If you're hungry, we could go somewhere."

"I'm fine now."

"What is this?" He took the glass again and drained it. "This didn't come out of my refrigerator."

"It's a healthy little concoction I like to drink."

"It's delicious. Health food usually tastes like medicine." He frowned.

Samara laughed. "Not all of them."

"Are you a health nut?"

"I don't think so. I try to eat right. I jog every day. Since I sit for a large part of my workday, I'd weigh a ton if I didn't do something."

"I jog, too. Usually behind the White House on the mall, although I rarely get the chance to sit when I'm at work."

"Things must be hectic there."

"They can be, but we're not going to talk about my work. I have something I want you to see that involves yours."

She raised her eyebrows and looked at him questioningly.

He stood. Samara got up and followed him to an upstairs bedroom. Justin opened the door and switched on the light. The room was empty. She went in. Leaning against the back wall was a huge canvas. She gasped at the beauty of it.

"Like it?" Justin asked softly. He put his hands on her shoulders and they both looked at the painting.

"It's beautiful. Where did you find it?" The painting

looked as if it were painted in the eighteenth century. It was a wedding scene. A bride and groom stood at the front of the cathedral. Light beams streamed in through cut-glass windows. The bride's head was turned to face her maid of honor and it appeared her train was caught on her bouquet as she handed it to the other woman. The scene was like a photo, a point in time that spoke of a lifetime of love.

"It's been in my family for a long time. I brought it back here after my sister got out of the hospital. It needs restoring. I hoped you would do it."

"Justin, I can't." She walked to the painting and knelt down in front of it.

"Why not?"

"I'm an apprentice. I studied painting in school, but I don't work with them. My restorations are on documents and it's more preservation than restoration. I've only worked on paintings a couple of times. You need a professional for this kind of thing. I can ask around and recommend someone."

She looked at him. He wasn't wearing a shirt and each time she saw his powerful frame, her body went hot. It was a good thing she was kneeling on the floor.

"My parents' fortieth anniversary is coming up. I want to restore the painting before that."

"*Forty years* together." She couldn't keep the incredulity out of her voice.

"Some people do mean it when they take their vows."

"Did you?"

He stared at her for a long moment. "I did at the time."

"That's just it. You can never be sure."

"There's no map to happily ever after, Samara. It's trust, love and wanting to make a life together. I wanted that when I got married. It didn't work out and we knew it. But it worked for my parents."

She turned back and stared at the painting. Her hands itched to touch it, to see it fully restored, with the colors as vibrant as they were when the artist finished it.

"Who painted this?" She looked in the corner, but saw no name.

"I don't know. Art is not my strong point, but my family loves this painting. And we'd all like to see it maintained."

Samara had been resting on her knees. She slid over and sat on the floor.

"Justin, something could happen to this. It's obviously worth a lot of money and certainly sentimental to your family. Is it insured?"

"I don't think so."

She dropped her head, then looked up at him. "Justin, someone could break in."

"It's pretty safe around here."

"There is no such thing. What would your parents think if something happened to this?"

"I know I need a security system," Justin conceded.

"You're a government employee, but in a very special role. For that alone, you should have a system. And being away so often is another reason to have one."

"All right," he said. "I'll call a service, but with my schedule, it's hard to know if I can be here long enough to allow someone to install a system."

"They do it in one day. Two at the most."

"I'll try."

She looked back at the painting. It was compelling, haunting even. The artist had translated the single moment, when two people entwined their lives, into a timeless expression of love. Samara was affected by it. She knew paintings, like poetry, were supposed to evoke emotion and this one did that job.

Justin did that, too. Whenever she looked at him, as she was doing now, admiring his body unclothed and darkly arousing, he evoked emotions that were as eternal as the painting.

If she could be sure that the way she felt now would continue through a lifetime together, she'd be more apt to trust combining her life with someone else's.

But, even with the painting in front of her and Justin close enough to share his body heat, she still had doubts.

Chapter 8

Weddings were haunting Samara. The painting at Justin's still called to her twenty-four hours later. And here she was walking down a runway surrounded by women in wedding gowns.

"This one is too gorgeous," Diana said. "I never thought this would be so much fun."

They'd been trying on the gowns they were going to model in the upcoming show, now only two weeks away. Samara didn't know how Geri had gotten the place set up and stocked in such a short time, but Geri often said she could do anything she wanted to do. Samara wondered if that applied to anyone or just to Geri.

"Samara, are you going to model the gown you have?" Diana asked.

"No, I am not," she answered firmly.

"Guys, you should see her in it."

"*See?* See her *in* it." Geri stopped rushing back and forth, taking care of every detail, to stare at Samara. "*You* had a wedding gown on?"

"And she looked *fan*tastic in it," Diana said. "It's the one from the trunk."

"The one you bought at the auction?" Carmen asked Samara.

"Same one," Diana answered. "I went to her place a couple nights ago to see the dress and who comes to the door with it on, but our Little Ms. Superstition."

"All right, can we get off of make-fun-of-Samara night?"

"I can't believe you tried the dress on," Carmen said.

"And I didn't die," Samara answered, frowning at her.

"Could I see it, Samara?" Geri asked. "Maybe it will fit into the show. An antique gown can't hurt business. Some brides want to wear their mother's or grandmother's gowns, but don't see how they can update them. Maybe there's something we can do."

"I'll bring it by tomorrow after work," she said, then remembered she'd agreed to meet Justin. "Oh, can't come tomorrow. I have something else to do."

"Does it involve *him?*" Diana asked shyly. She was obviously into dropping bombshells tonight. And it worked. Her friends all stared at her, waiting for an answer.

"As a matter of fact, my date is with a painting—an old painting." She glared at Diana.

"I might have thought it was something like that," Carmen said, with disappointment.

"Okay. Never mind. Try it again," Geri instructed. "Samara, walk down the runway."

Standing up straight, wearing a bright yellow, off-the-shoulder dress, Samara took a step and paraded down the narrow path to the end. She turned several times and walked back, stopping in the center to make one more set of turns.

"That's good. I need the wedding gowns now."

Diana, Carmen and Shane took their positions. Shane went first. Geri described the dress as she walked down the runway. Samara watched. She was regal and for a moment Samara imagined herself in the gown.

"Geri, where are the other models? You have a ton of dresses here. The three of us can't model them all. We don't change that fast."

"I contacted a local modeling school. The students came during the day. They were glad to get a real opportunity to work."

Shane nodded.

"Besides, with them here, we can't talk like we have been." Geri looked at Samara.

"Maybe they should have been here. Then you all wouldn't be attacking me," Samara said.

"Samara, we're not attacking you," Geri said. "You know we're in your corner."

"Yeah," Carmen said. "I know I can be brash sometimes—"

"Sometimes?" Samara said.

"Well, more than not," she said. "But you make yourself such an easy target." Shane walked down the front steps of the runway and hugged Samara. "But I'd come any distance if you needed my help."

"I know that." She looked up and Geri, Diana and Carmen were standing in support. Samara felt the love of her friends. She knew they would always be there. Just as she was there for them. She'd do whatever was necessary to help any one of them.

After a moment, Geri broke away. "Now that the group hug is out of the way, could we get back to the task at hand?"

"Leave it to Geri to send us all back to work," Diana said with a laugh.

They went back to the gowns and getting used to going up and down the few steps to get on and off the runway.

"You'll never guess whom I talked to today," Geri said, as she watched them walking back and forth.

They waited for her to tell them. It appeared she wanted them to guess.

"Don't keep us in suspense, who was it?" Shane asked.

"Callie Stevens."

"Who's Callie Stevens?" Carmen asked.

"You remember her. You met her at the mall art festival about two years ago," Geri explained. "Her real name is Allison Stevens."

"Is she the one who's married to that strange guy with the whiny voice?"

"That's the one," Samara said.

"I remember her now," Carmen said, light seeming to dawn in her brain. "What did she call for?"

"She heard about the store. Apparently, she and Mr. Whiny Voice are divorced. She's about to marry, *again.* This time to Eddie Winston. He graduated high school with us and they want to have their reception at Shadow Walk. I can't believe my old classmates are divorcing and marrying each other. This is the third one I've heard of in the last six months."

"There must be something to this marriage thing if they are all doing it multiple times," Diana joked.

Samara thought she was speaking directly to her. She also thought of Justin's parents. Forty years together. The bond between their generation must be made of cement, while Samara's generation's bonds had the consistency of kindergarten paste.

The door to Justin's house swung inward as Samara scurried up the steps. He stood in the doorway, waiting for her. As she reached him, he swept her into his arms and kissed her. Samara didn't know how her heart survived the constant slamming against her chest whenever she thought of him.

As soon as he'd called, asking her to come over, the drum beat launched inside her. When Justin's arms clasped around her like giant heat bands and his mouth seared hers, her heart thudded even harder. Memories of their night together flooded her brain, sending her body into overdrive, and she wanted to repeat the miracle.

He held her, bending her backward, his mouth plundering hers until she didn't think she could stand it any longer. She clung to him, her arms around his neck, her body aligned with his. He lifted his mouth and groaned.

"I'm sure this job isn't worth it," he said, his voice lower than normal.

"What job?" Samara knew she shouldn't ask, but she hadn't mastered the art of Washington secrecy yet.

"That's why I called you. I have to go to work and there's an army of workmen here. I thought you could oversee them while I'm away. You know what needs to be done."

At that moment, Samara heard the hammering and voices coming from upstairs. She looked up as a woman came down the stairs. She was wearing a blue workman's jumpsuit. She had a tool belt around her waist and her hair was knotted on top of her head.

"Mr. Beckett?" she said when she reached the bottom step. She looked at Samara.

"This is Ms. Scott," Justin introduced her. "I have to go to work. She'll answer any questions you have and explain exactly what's needed."

"Amy Rogers." The woman stretched her hand out and Samara shook it. Her palm was calloused and rough to the touch.

"Amy is from Prince George's Security. She's the crew supervisor."

"I wanted to ask about the basement windows," Amy said.

Justin spread his hands. "I have to go now. You can handle it," he said to Samara.

And with a quick kiss dropped onto her mouth, he was gone. Samara looked after him. She loved watching him. Whether he was coming toward her or walking away, the power of his confidence was evident. He commanded attention.

Turning back, she noticed Amy was still behind her. "Let's go see what's in the basement," Samara said, covering the distraction on her senses that Justin produced. Her mind saw the bedroom and the two of them entwined in each other's arms. Her body felt his weight pressing her into scented sheets. She had to break the connection and discovering a silent Amy Rogers watching her intently, Samara forced herself to find something innocuous to think about. Basement windows won.

Sometimes dreams really did come true. Justin hoped Samara would still be at his house when he got back. Never knowing when that might be, he wasn't sure if she would take the chance of waiting. But he found her there, sleeping on the sofa.

He leaned against the doorjamb, his arms folded, watching her. He liked coming home to someone who was waiting up for him. He grinned. Even if "waiting up" meant she'd fallen asleep.

Pushing away from the door, he advanced to the sofa and sat down. Her legs were warm against him. She stirred, but didn't wake. Justin leaned forward and ran his hand over her hair and down her cheek.

Her eyes opened and she smiled as they focused on him.

"Hi," she said, her voice sleepy and sexy.

"Hi," he answered. "I'm glad you stayed."

"Someone had to show you how to set the alarm."

"Is that the only reason?"

"What else could there be?" The sound of her voice implied the opposite of her words.

He smiled and leaned forward and kissed her.

"Did everything go all right? At work?" she asked.

He nodded with a sigh. "Another *world crisis* averted."

"I'm glad to hear that."

He looked at her and realized she was frightened. Was that why she'd stayed, more than to show him the operation of the security system?

"What happens if there is a world crisis?" she asked.

He glanced away, knowing there was no way to answer that question. It depended on what the crisis was. There were scenarios written and updated every day for any possibility that they could think of, but he was duty-bound to keep what he knew to himself.

He gathered her close, hugging her to him. "I can't answer that."

"If there was a crisis, would you be in any danger?"

"I don't think so," he said.

He wouldn't be in the line of fire, but he'd be a major advisor. And in today's world, even the advisors could be targets.

"Did everything go all right here?" He changed the subject.

She leaned back and looked in his eyes. Justin knew she was assessing whether he was being truthful with her.

"I'll be fine," he assured her. "Now, tell me about the alarm system."

She got up and walked him through the various codes and zones the control panel affected.

"So the painting is safe now?"

"Not only the painting. You're safer, too."

He wondered if the system had been more about protecting him than protecting a painting. Was there a crack in her armor? Was he getting through the casing she had around her and finding a place in her heart? He hoped so.

"And speaking of the painting. I spoke to one of the restoration experts at work about the painting. She recommended someone who might be available to clean and restore it."

"That's good news."

"I had him come by and look at the painting. He thinks it only needs a little cleaning and that it can be done in a short period of time."

Justin smiled. "More good news."

"He can only work a couple of nights a week and on

weekends, but he doesn't think it will take very long. He wants to come Monday night."

"I'm not going to be here until late. I'll have to give you a key."

"What?" She stepped away from him, standing up straighter than she already was. "I don't want a key."

"Relax," he said. "It's just for the painting. You can give it back to me when the job is done."

"Justin, I know we moved a little fast, but it's not time for keys yet. You don't really know me."

"Are you a serial killer?"

"Of course not."

"Are you a thief?"

"Only to lonely hearts."

Justin winked at her. "Are you a *lobbyist?*" He grinned, lowering his voice on the last word and making an awful face.

"No." Samara laughed, too.

"What about a forger, specifically of art, not documents?"

She shook her head.

"Then I would say it's all right if you oversee this project. Of course, I could hire you as project manager. Then it would all be legitimate." His smile was teasing. "But how would that look when we spend the night together?"

"I think I'd better go," she said.

"Why?"

"Because you're losing your mind and I don't want to be here for it."

He walked to where she stood. She didn't move. He watched her head come up as his taller physique moved closer.

"I am losing my mind," he said. "Over you."

His arms circled her waist. Pulling her into contact with his body opened a heat duct within him. He was falling for her and falling hard. He kissed her tenderly, his mouth brushing over hers. He wanted to crush her to him, but he forced himself to hold off, to keep his embrace affectionate.

When the kiss ended, he held her for a long time. His arms banded across her back. He wanted to go on holding her forever, but knew that wasn't possible. At least not yet. There were things she needed to learn and understand. He knew she didn't believe in happily ever after. And there was no way he could guarantee her that.

All he could do was show her how things could be. And he vowed that he would do just that. Lifting her feet from the floor, her head rested on his shoulder, her arms around his neck. He turned toward the stairs and the bedroom.

Restoring a painting was hard work and took special equipment. It couldn't be done at Justin's house. They had to move it to a facility that was set up for this kind of work. Harry Candlewick was the man that had been recommended to her. He worked with an independent team of conservators and had made arrangements for

Samara to assist him in working on the painting at his offices in Maryland.

He arrived Monday night with a truck equipped to secure and move the canvas. As they angled the huge frame through the door, a car pulled in and parked behind Harry's truck. A man got out.

"Excuse me," he shouted. "What are you doing?"

Samara recognized him from the picture she'd seen in Justin's great room.

"You're one of Justin's brothers," she said. "I've met Christian. I'm Samara Scott, a friend of Justin's."

"Austin Beckett," he said.

Austin was about the same height as his brother, but there the resemblance ended. While Justin was tall and lanky, Austin was solid muscle. Justin's hair was short and neat, while Austin's was longer and braided. Two-inch-long plaits covered his scalp in a neat pattern. He was dressed in a business suit.

"Chicago." She remembered. "He told me you live in Chicago."

"I'm here for the day and thought I'd see if Justin was home. He didn't answer his cell, but then it's catch-as-catch-can when he does. Where are you taking the painting? It belongs to my parents."

"This is Harry Candlewick. He's a conservator. We're going to clean and restore the painting for your parents. Justin tells me it's their fortieth anniversary." Justin hadn't said he wanted the painting done for that, but Samara thought he probably did.

"If you know that much, I guess you're legitimate."
He shook hands with Harry.

"Let us load this and I'll give you a card," Harry said.
They put the painting in the truck and secured it. Then
Harry and Samara jumped out of the back and Harry pro-
duced a card. "This is where we're taking the painting."

"I take it he's not inside?"

"Work," Samara answered. If Austin knew his
brother well enough, he'd know that work took up most
of his time.

"Do you know when he'll be home?"

Samara shook her head. "His hours are irregular. He
said he'd be late tonight. I have no idea what time."

"I have a key, I'll wait for him. Nice meeting you both."

He walked toward the front door. Samara suddenly
remembered the alarm.

"Austin," she called and ran toward him. "There's an
alarm system. I'll have to let you in."

Producing the key Justin had given her, she opened
the door and disabled the alarm.

"Thanks," he said. "I guess you mean a lot to Justin."

The television droned on with some program Samara
wasn't really listening to. Next to her sat a glass of soda
and bowl of popcorn. In her hand were the keys Justin
had given her, trusted her with.

Austin's words had rung in her ears for the rest of the
day and night. What was her role with Justin? What had
she allowed? She and Justin certainly made beautiful

music together. And she was more than his restorer, but where did it end? Usually relationships progressed to the next level, meeting, dating, intimacy, marriage... She stopped. She'd made it clear that she was not interested in going that far.

And Justin had accepted that.

Or did he?

Did she?

Somewhere along the way, it seemed the lines had blurred. She couldn't remember a line at all when he was in her presence. When his arms were around her, there was not only an absence of lines, but an absence of everything else except the all-consuming nature of their joining.

Samara was unsure what was happening to her. Each time he held her in his arms, she forgot her convictions, forgot the statistics she so often spouted. She needed to be consistent, to push back, stand by her thoughts and let Justin know that there wasn't anything more between them.

Snapping her hand closed around the keys, she picked up the phone and called him. As usual, she got his machine. She snapped the receiver back in place and got up. The keys would let her into the house and she already had the alarm code. She would leave the keys and that would be enough of a message for him.

Arriving a few minutes later, the lights were on inside. She rang the bell and waited. Justin came to the door.

"What a surprise," he said, a broad smile covering his

dark brown face. "I wasn't expecting you." The smile disappeared when he saw the look on hers. "What's wrong?"

"I brought your keys." She stretched her open hand toward him.

Justin looked at the keys as if she were holding a serpent toward him. Finally he reached out and took them. In the same action, he took her hand. Pulling her across the threshold, he led her into the great room and pushed her into a chair. He took the one opposite her. "What happened?" he asked.

"Nothing."

"Then why are you angry?"

"I'm not angry." But she was. She was angry with herself. Angry that she'd given herself a set of standards and she was not living by them. She'd allowed her convictions to be smudged, rubbed out, almost forgotten. But she would no longer do that. Their relationship had gone as far as it could go. It was time for them to part.

"My brother told me he met you."

She nodded.

"Did he say anything that caused this anger?"

"I am not angry," she shouted.

Justin waited a moment. She could see he was controlling his frustration. He'd probably had a hard day at work, if he'd gone there. And her being less-than-forthcoming was probably driving him crazy. Samara didn't know how to say it. On the drive here she'd rehearsed what she was going to say if she found him home, but the moment he opened the door her resolve deserted her.

"Austin and I had dinner together," he began. "He said nice things about you, called you beautiful. Most of our other conversation centered around family. Then he had to catch a plane and return to Chicago. He told me you were moving the painting when he arrived."

"I'm sorry about that. Apparently, you didn't need the alarm system, at least not for the painting. Once Harry determined what had to be done, we needed more equipment than could be brought in. Austin thought we were stealing it."

"I know. He's lived in Chicago too long. He suspects everyone."

"He was right to be suspicious," she smiled, tentatively. "Does your family often drop in like that?"

He shook his head. "They know my hours are erratic. Austin called, but I couldn't answer the phone."

"It was good you got to spend time with him."

"We enjoy each other's company."

"I'm glad," she said. "Families should be close."

"We are. As are you and your sister. Now please tell me what this is about? The day has been long."

Samara stood up. Justin did the same. "I won't keep you," she told him. "I came to return the keys. I won't be needing them."

"Samara, what happened?" He put his hands out to touch her, stop her from leaving, but he dropped them to his sides. Samara communicated that touching her wasn't the right course of action.

"I think we should slow things down a bit," she said.

"Slow them or drop them?"

She stared at him. "Drop them," she said.

"Why? I at least deserve to know why."

She said nothing.

"Is it my job? Not being available? Not being reliable?"

"Justin, I told you at the beginning that you should find someone else. Someone who appreciates your attention."

"You don't? I'd stake my life on that being a lie."

"Lie or not, do it." She started for the door. She expected him to follow her. To call out for her to stop.

But he didn't.

Chapter 9

Leaving Justin was the easy part. Removing him from her mind was hard. Especially when she returned to her desk after a late afternoon meeting and found an envelope lying on top of it. She knew there was a postcard inside it. The handwriting was Justin's. She'd have recognized it from across the room.

Samara refused to open it. She should throw it in the trash. They were slowing things down. Ending things. This was not the way to end things. Turning around, she entered her workroom. The low-lighted room had a large table on which lay a letter from 1879. Usually she felt a rush working on old documents. Stories ran through her head about the people who had written them, what their lives were like. But lately all she thought of was Justin.

What would the person working in this office think of the postcards a hundred years from now? How would she or he interpret the handwriting on the card? The strong strokes of the pen. The way he formed the bowl of the *S* that began her name. The long, continuing line that extended from the final *A?* Would they think they were lovers that met, meshed, married and lived into dotage together? Would they know they were destined to part, that the forces pulling them apart were greater than any that could keep them together?

Samara turned back, returning to her desk and snatching up the envelope. She tore it open, not taking the time to slit it as she usually did with a letter opener.

On the cover was the picture of a chest. Unlike the other cards, the antique-look on this one was probably genuine. The chest was made of dark wood and intricately carved. Samara sat down when she saw it. It was beautiful.

The message read: *I don't know much about hope chests, but I have HOPE.* Samara dropped the card. She'd never been pursued like this. A streak of guilt went through her. She didn't understand it. She'd tried his method. It hadn't worked. And wouldn't. Better to end it now, she told herself.

Justin was unreliable. His job came first and that was both a virtue and a curse. He couldn't be counted on to sit through a play. What would happen if something really important came up? But he *was* persistent—and gorgeous—but more than his physical appearance, he was a kind, loving man. She smiled, remembering Justin's dimple in his left cheek. She'd often wanted to trace it with her finger. Picking up the card, her fingers stroked the paper with the same tenderheartedness she would use if it was Justin's face.

Hope, she thought. It was a single word. But one that could hold the world together.

It would be good if she could make a clean break of it, forget him and never think of him again, but they had shared too much. His kisses tingled against her lips, even though he wasn't there. She could feel the impression of his body holding hers. And, there was the painting. She still had to work on that. Each time she looked at it, there would be his face imposed over every inch of the paint.

And it would begin tonight. She was meeting Harry in an hour. Gathering her things, she cleaned up and took the elevator to the lobby floor. Alan Stackhouse was in his usual position by the door as she approached it.

"Good night, Alan," she said, opening her briefcase for his inspection.

He gave the contents a cursory look. "Thank you," he said. "Did you get your letter?"

"You put the letter on my desk?"

"No, ma'am. I saw Mr. Hargraves. I asked him to deliver it."

There were security guards all over the building, all

with different levels of clearance. Alan wasn't allowed below this floor.

"He left it for me," she said. "Thank you."

He nodded. With a smile, he said, "Have a nice evening."

Samara went out into the evening air. Justin hadn't heeded her warning. He'd enlisted Alan as his emissary.

She tried to put Justin out of her mind, but she kept running into things that reminded her of him. Like the painting. It was the first thing she saw when she got to Harry's office. He'd removed the frame and the painting sat exposed on a large table. Harry stood, studying it. He wasn't applying any of the cleaning techniques he'd told her about. He seemed to be in another world.

"Does it remind you of anything?" Harry asked.

Samara stared at it, trying to see anything out of the ordinary. She shook her head. "Art is not my strong suit. I can pick out a master, but I'm not good on other painters."

"I've seen this before," he said. "Or at least something like it."

"What?"

"I can't quite pull it into focus, but my mind tells me this is familiar." He hunched his shoulders and seemed to drop the subject. "Next time you talk to Justin, ask him where he got this."

"He said it's been in his family for decades."

"Let's get to work."

They had already photographed and X-rayed the painting to see if there were previous restorations. There appeared to be three distinct layers of protective lining under the original canvas. These were removed leaving the original canvas exposed. When the final layer was removed and the back of the painting exposed, the dried adhesive resembled coarse sandpaper. Samara used a scalpel and a rough brush to laboriously clean it away. The job was tedious and tiring. She and Harry worked slowly to avoid any damage.

It took hours to do it, but when they finished, both were ready to let the next phase wait for another day. As they washed up and prepared to leave, there was a knock at the door.

Harry went to see who it was. While he was gone, Samara noticed something on the backing they had removed. She recognized words. They were written in German. She couldn't read them, but she looked closer at them.

About to call Harry, her voice stuck in her throat when he came through the door followed by Justin.

"What are you doing here?" Samara asked, not even disguising the surprise in her voice.

"I thought you might need a ride home."

She wanted to ask him how he knew where she was or that they were finished for the night, but with Harry standing between them, she merely smiled.

"See you Thursday," Harry said. "Same time."

Samara had no choice but to leave with Justin. On the street, Harry said good-night and they went toward their cars.

"Justin, you shouldn't have come."

"The streets are dangerous," he said. "You told me that. I'm here for your safety."

They reached the car. He put his hand on the door handle, but didn't open it.

"The truth is I miss seeing you."

Samara looked up at him. The light from the parking lot lamps gave her a clear vision of his face. She saw sincerity in his eyes, along with need and what she thought was hope.

"I got your postcard," she told him.

"Is there any hope?"

Looking at him was her undoing. She had the words that needed to be said ready to utter, but voicing them was something she was incapable of doing. Hope was in his eyes. She couldn't kill it. She knew there was hope inside her, too.

Reaching up, she brushed her hand along his face, one finger lingering at the dimple in his left cheek. When his head bowed toward hers, she went up on her toes to meet him. Their mouths melded like long-lost lovers. Her arms went around his neck and her body moved to align with his of its own volition. How could she have thought she could stop this bond they had? He called it *chemistry,* but it had to be something stronger than that.

He occupied her thoughts night and day. She thought of his smile, his teasing ways and the world-changing way he made love to her.

"We have to get out of this parking lot," Justin said.

Samara had forgotten where they were. Jerkily, she got into the car.

"How did you know where I was?" she asked when they were driving back toward the District.

"I called your apartment and you didn't answer."

"I had my cell."

"I wasn't sure you'd answer if I called the cell."

His name and number would come up on the display and Samara would know who was calling before she answered. She also had Caller ID on her apartment phone, but she didn't mention that.

"I had the card Harry gave my brother. When I left work, I drove up here."

"Harry asked about the painting's origin."

"Asked what?"

"He says it reminds him of something."

"Another painting?"

"I think so. He wondered where your family got it."

"I don't know. It's just always been there. I'll ask my father." He stopped at a red light and glanced at her. "By the way, will you go with me to their anniversary party?"

"Are you sure you'll be there?"

His gesture showed he understood exactly what she meant. "I know we had a couple of mishaps, but a lot is going on at work and things are changing. I'm not missing the anniversary. So can I count on you?"

"Justin, hadn't we said we'd slow this down?"

"We did. The party isn't for a couple of months. Is that slow enough for you?"

Samara knew she was going to go with him the moment he asked. She wanted to see him, be with him more than anything. Even her convictions couldn't keep her from agreeing.

She nodded.

The e-mail popped up on her screen Thursday afternoon. Samara saw Harry's address and opened it immediately. They were supposed to meet that night. If he couldn't make it, he would let her know. But that wasn't it.

The note said for her to look at the link he had embedded in the message. Clicking on it, up came a photo of the painting they were restoring. Samara read the story attached to it. Horror went through her as she read. She remembered the German words on the backing.

The painting was German war bounty.

She hit the print button and grabbed the phone at the same time. Calling Justin's cell, she left him a message that she wanted to see him tonight.

He texted her back almost immediately with the time he expected to pick her up. It would be late, but he asked her to wait for him.

Samara had been waiting for an hour when he finally picked her up and pulled in front of his house and parked. She got out of the car and they went right into his house.

"Are you all right?" he asked.

"I'm fine. It's not me."

"What is it, then?"

"It's the painting."

"Can't it be restored?"

"That's not it." Samara paused.

"I asked you once where you got it," she said. They had reached his kitchen. She sat on one of the chairs at the table.

"And I told you."

"We've found out a little more about it. Harry recognized it."

"What do you mean he recognized it?"

"He sent me an Internet link this afternoon. When I opened the file, the exact painting was there."

"So there's a copy on the Internet. What does that mean?"

Samara stared at him. "Justin, the painting is German war bounty. You have to give it back to the original owner."

"That painting has been in my family for decades. There must be some mistake."

She handed him the papers. He took them and started reading. After a moment he sat down at the kitchen table.

"There's got to be a mistake. That painting has hung at our house for as long as I can remember."

"You've got to find the true owner," she told him. "Think of your reputation. You're a lawyer working for a critical Washington agency whose purpose is shrouded in mystery. Your actions have got to be aboveboard. Or they could—"

"Go a lot further up than you can imagine," he finished. "I'll have it checked out." He took her hands. "I

promise. There's nothing I can do about it tonight."
Dropping her hand, he looked at his watch. "Saturday,
we'll go on a hunting trip and clear up any doubt in your
mind. Will that work?"

Samara nodded.

Justin made no overtures to keep Samara in his house,
although he wanted to with all his heart. Suppressing his
wishes, he took her back to the car. Opening the door,
Samara slid into the seat. Crossing the front of the car,
Justin got in beside her. After the way she left him the night
before, he didn't think he'd see her again. But he took the
chance and had the guard deliver a postcard for him.

It represented hope and Justin had hope for them. He
felt she was special, that what was happening between
them was special. He knew he needed to take things
slowly. He hadn't wined and dined her the way he
wanted to. Each time he tried, his job got in the way.

But that was about the change.

"Tired?" Justin asked Samara.

"Exhausted," she said: "I never knew pouring over a
painting could be so tiring."

He started the engine. "I'll take you home," Justin said.

Samara rested her head against the back of the seat
as Justin pulled into traffic. In moments she was asleep.
Justin wished he could drive for hours, keeping her next
to him. Her apartment came up much too fast. He parked
and leaned over to look at her. After a moment she
stirred and opened her eyes.

"Are we there already?" she asked, blinking. Pushing herself up in the seat, she reached for her purse that had slipped to the floor.

Justin got out and walked around the car. He helped her out and silently they entered the building. At her door, she stepped inside. He hung back. She turned, questioning his decision.

"Aren't you coming in?" she asked.

He shook his head. "Don't imagine for a moment that I don't want to do just that," he told her. "But you're tired and not totally in control of yourself. You said we should slow down. I'm trying to do that."

She stared at him, but said nothing. Justin wondered what she was thinking. He knew he wanted to hold her through the night, wanted to feel her body against his, but morning would come and with it the chance that if she had been less vulnerable, things wouldn't have gone so far.

"See you Saturday morning," he said.

She nodded. "Thanks for coming tonight. And thanks for looking into the painting." Samara smiled, then going up on her toes, she kissed his cheek, her mouth lingering with a promise that Justin wasn't sure was implied. She could be grateful. She could be tired. Or she could want him as much as he wanted her.

Justin felt as if he would melt. He had to force his arms from savagely pulling Samara into him. Samara's mouth left his cheek and slid across his lips. What was she doing? His boiling point was low where she was concerned. Her arms went around his waist and she pressed into him.

"Sam, what are you doing?"

She answered with her mouth. Like a jackknife his hands moved around her, embraced her, forcing her forward. His mouth came down on hers as if she were a drug he couldn't live without. He pressed her to him, his hands running the course of her, learning her curves, feeling the warmth of her, feeling the arousal in himself.

His tongue pressed between her teeth. She opened to his invasion like a flower to a new day. For him it was a new day. He was in love with her. He held her close and never wanted to let her go. He wanted her next to him for the good days to come, for the bad days they would get through together. He wanted to love her, offer her a life filled with a love so intense, so tender and so raw that she would never be in doubt that she was truly loved, cherished and needed.

Samara's arms were tight around his neck, her body soft as it matched the length of his. He pressed her back against the door, outlining her mouth with his tongue, blocking her face with his hands, reeling from the way she carried him from anything logical in the world and into their own special place. He groaned against her mouth, wanting beyond all reason, to go where her body was leading him, but he'd promised himself to slow things down.

With an effort he didn't know he possessed, he eased his mouth from hers. Her head dropped to his shoulder and she hung in his arms, as limp as a living doll. Her breasts heaved against his chest as she took life-breathing oxygen into her lungs. Justin stroked her arms, pulling her from the door behind her and caressing her back. His hands went up into her hair and he kissed her temples before pushing her into her apartment and pulling the door closed.

He heard the lock click into place and walked down the hall toward the elevator. His heart was happy and he felt like whistling, but all his effort was used up as he focused on walking a straight line.

The sun shone brightly Saturday morning and there was a soft breeze. Samara met Justin as he pulled into the circular driveway of her apartment building. She opened the passenger door and got into the car.

Justin leaned over and kissed her briefly. Then he came back for a long, lingering kiss. Drawing her seat belt, she fixed it in place, giving herself time to get used to breathing in Justin's presence. He had the power to make her forget everything when he was near.

Starting the car, he merged into the morning traffic on Sixteenth Street.

"Where are we going?" Samara asked, something she hadn't thought to do before.

"My parents' house," Justin answered.

"What?" she said, snapping her head around to look at him.

"It's the best place to start. They own the painting."

"I know, but…"

"What?" he asked.

Samara didn't know how to express her feelings. The last place she wanted to go was to his family's home.

"I thought we were going to a library, or an art gallery."

"Maybe, but we'll start there."

"That's hours away."

"We'll be back by nightfall."

"What happens if you get a call to go to work?"

"I won't. My last day at OEO was yesterday."

"What? Why?"

"It's time someone else saved the world. Or at least the United States." He smiled, taking the edge off his words. "I've moved to the EEOB." Eisenhower Executive Office Building, a huge French Second Empire style, gray stone structure adjacent to the West Wing. "I've joined the White House legal staff. I start in a week."

"That's wonderful," Samara said. She was genuinely happy for him.

"It means somewhat normal hours."

"Normal? You'll be working for the White House."

"Yeah, but even the president sleeps sometimes. There is a large staff, so I'm not on twenty-four-hour call. And if I make a date with you, I'll be able to keep it. Like today."

"I did wonder if you would make it or if I'd be standing at the end of the walkway, waiting and waiting."

"No more of that."

"Did you ask for this change?"

He nodded.

"Did it have anything to do with me?"

"Maybe. But if you did, it was in an indirect way. I didn't apply for the change because of you." He glanced at her, then turned his attention back to the traffic. "Although you would be a good reason for wanting more suitable hours, I doubt they would have hired me because of that."

"I'm crushed." She smiled.

Justin reached over and squeezed her hand, then released it.

"Being on the EEOB legal staff is a promotion. I can use what I learned working at OEO in the new position and I'll have more normal hours. At OEO you exist at the highest levels all the time. You can't do that for very long. You burn out. I wanted to move before that happened."

"Do you get to rub elbows with the president now?"

"Afraid not. I'm still too far down on the totem pole for that. I think the new staff will get to meet him for a photo op, but that's it."

"Congratulations. I'm happy for you."

"Thanks." For a few minutes Justin drove in silence. Samara watched the city roll away and the landscape change to trees and woods.

"Tell me about your family," she said, turning back to him.

"You met two of my brothers. My sister runs a small company. She's an animator, does freelance work for some of the biggest companies in the U.S. She has her own children's program on PBS."

"That sounds interesting. Is she fully recovered from her accident?"

He nodded. "She's a trooper. No ill effects the doctors say."

"What's the name of the children's program?"

"The Wilson Cousins. It's about—"

"I know it," she interrupted with a smile. "Your sister writes that?"

"Writes, directs, produces, animates, you name it."

"What about Micah? He's the brother that lives in Maryland?"

Justin nodded. "If you asked him, he'd tell you he was just a marine."

"A marine in western Maryland? There's no marine base in western Maryland. The only military facility out here is—" She stopped as the impact of what she was about to say weighed on her. "Camp David. Your brother protects the president?"

"No, but he is stationed at the Camp."

"You have a very impressive family," Samara told him. "Your parents must be very proud."

"They are. And they're looking forward to meeting you."

"You told them about me?" she asked, surprised.

"When I told them I was bringing you home, they naturally had questions."

Of course, they would, Samara thought. "Justin, I'm going to investigate the painting, not on approval as a future daughter-in-law."

"I understand that."

She wondered if he did. He didn't act like it. But then the clues she gave him weren't those of a woman in a business relationship with a man. As soon as she said it, her actions spoke a different language. And as much as Justin said he believed her, understood her position, she knew he didn't. Inside he thought she would change, that her conviction had changed, that she didn't really believe it any longer.

Samara wondered if that was true. A few minutes ago he'd told her he was in a job that had normal hours. Her heart raced. When he said there would be future dates, it pounded loud enough for him to hear it.

And now as the car sped along the road toward Maryland, she had the feeling she was not going to verify the ownership of a painting.

She was meeting the family.

Chapter 10

Fear and apprehension evaporated the moment Samara stepped inside Justin's family home. The house was huge, but the family made it cozy and welcoming. His father was a man of letters. A professor of English at the College of Cumberland. Lane Beckett had a large library and enjoyed reading. Samara had a long conversation with him on working with old documents and some of the specific ones she'd seen and handled. Before she knew it, he was inviting her to guest-lecture at some of his classes when the new semester started in September.

"Give her a rest," Justin's mother said, coming into the library, carrying a tray. "Samara, he will talk your head off. He can't wait to get back to the classroom where he has a captive audience."

"I find him fascinating," she said.

"That's because this is the first time you've heard his stories."

Lane got up and kissed his wife on the temple. He patted her arm affectionately as he did it. Samara watched them. Her own parents did not have this kind of relationship. Lane and Katie were married forty years and they still had a love for each other that she could see. If Samara ever married, she'd want that kind of love.

Justin and his sister, Deanna, came in. The doorbell rang as they sat down.

"That would be Micah," Deanna said. "I'll get it."

She came back on the arm of a tall guy in uniform. Samara had seen many military guys, but his presence was so commanding she thought she should stand up.

"This is my brother, Michael," Justin introduced, pumping his hand. "We call him Micah." Michael stepped forward as Samara offered her hand. His swallowed hers like it was a whale eating a minnow.

"Justin speaks well of you."

Samara smiled and glanced at Justin, wondering what he had said about her.

"I thought we were going horseback riding," Deanna said to her brother. "You don't appear to be dressed for it." She looked her brother up and down.

"I have a change of clothes upstairs, but I have to be back at the base by morning."

"How about you, Samara, do you ride?" Micah asked.

"She's not here for that," Justin said. "We need to talk to Mom and Dad."

"Sounds interesting."

"It's about the painting."

"The wedding painting?" Deanna asked.

"I'm cleaning it," Samara explained. "During the process we found an indication that it might have been…" She trailed off.

"She thinks it's German war bounty," Justin finished for her.

"That old painting?" Deanna said.

"War?" Micah said, simultaneously, his voice authoritative. Samara was sure she saw his shoulders straightened a little more—if that was possible.

"My father bought that painting," Lane said. "We have the papers."

"That's what I want to show her," Justin said. "They prove the painting is ours and Samara won't have any misgivings about working on it. Where are they, Dad?"

"I think they're in one of those trunks up in the attic. We stored a lot of stuff there after my dad died," Lane said.

"Why don't you go change, Micah? I'll go look for the papers," Justin suggested.

"I wanted to talk to you about something," Micah addressed his brother.

"Then I'll help find them," Deanna said.

"As I remember, they're in an envelope with your grandmother's handwriting on it," her father said.

"I'm not sure I can recognize Grandma's handwriting. What does it say?"

"Something about a wedding. Probably the title of the painting."

"Come on, Samara. It's just us girls looking for a wedding." She laughed at her own joke.

Samara had started to get up, but Deanna's words cut her at the knees and she fell back into the chair. On a second try she got up, hoping no one saw her reaction.

The four of them went up the stairs. The guys stopped on the second level and Samara followed Deanna up another flight of stairs.

"Are you completely recovered from your accident?" Samara asked. "Justin told me you were critical for a while."

"I was cleaning windows at my company. I'll never do that again." She looked over her shoulder at Samara. "When I fell I cut an artery in my leg. I was lucky I didn't bleed to death. I still get a little tired, but the doctors said I could return to my normal routine."

"That's good."

"It would be if you didn't have a family like this one. They watch me like hawks, making sure I'm not overdoing."

"That's because they love you."

She stopped at the top. "I know. I love them, too, and I'd be sad if they did anything less." She smiled and turned to open a door.

The attic was finished and divided into several

rooms. The space was clean and dust-free, although it smelled a little musty.

Deanna looked around pensively. "Where should we start?"

Samara had no idea. She looked around. "Are there any files?"

"That's something we never brought up here."

"Your father said there were trunks."

"They're over here." Deanna moved toward a door. When she opened it, Samara saw more than a few trunks. The room was full of them. Some had names on them. Some were steamer trunks. Samara had never seen a steamer trunk outside of an old movie.

"We each had a different one when we went off to college. This was mine." Deanna sat on a footlocker. "That one belonged to Micah. You can tell. It's still as clean as a marine."

They both laughed. Samara looked around, trying to identify the one that belonged to Justin.

"This one," Deanna told her. "This is Justin's."

Samara followed Deanna's gaze. "It looks like it's been around the world."

"It has. Justin studied in Oxford, Paris, South Africa, the Middle East, Japan. Hasn't he told you?"

Samara shook her head. Now she understood why he worked for OEO. "I suppose he's gotten used to keeping things to himself. It's an occupational hazard when you work for the government."

Deanna opened a trunk and looked inside. She closed

it, deciding that wasn't the one. Samara pitched in and helped. The fifth trunk they opened had old photograph albums in it. Deanna pulled one out. "I'd forgotten about these," she said sitting down on the floor and opening the huge cover. She pointed to an old photo. "This is my great-grandmother."

Samara looked down. The photo was sepia-colored and included a stern-looking man and a woman with the shadow of a smile on her face.

"From what I've heard, she was quite a woman. But look at her husband. What a sourpuss." Deanna looked up. "In those days few people smiled in photos. Some superstition or other told them to look stern." Deanna demonstrated, putting a stern look on her face. The action made Samara laugh. "But great-granny here was defiant even on film."

Glancing into the trunk, Samara saw another album, one with a photo of a couple on the cover. She picked it up and opened it. Inside she found a photo of the bride alone.

"What a beautiful gown," she whispered to herself, but Deanna heard her and turned to see what she was looking at.

"That's my grandmother," she said. "I love that photo. The dress is over there."

Samara looked up, but saw nothing.

"It's in the other room."

They got up and went through the door. Walking through the main room, she opened a door at the end and switched on a light. The gown stood on a dress form inside a glass case.

Samara gasped. It was almost as if a person was standing there.

"Sorry," Deanna apologized. "I should have warned you. When I was little and we used to play up here, coming upon the dress like this would scare me, too, especially when the room was dark."

"It's more beautiful than it is in the photo. My friend Geri would love to see this." Samara glanced at Deanna. "She's opening a bridal shop and having a fashion show as a grand-opening event. I'm one of her models."

"That's great. Why don't you try it on? It looks like it would fit."

"No." Samara stepped back as if she'd been hit. "I couldn't do it. It's in a glass case."

"That's just to keep it clean." Deanna dismissed her reservations. "And to satisfy my mother. She found the case at a going-out-of-business sale and put the dress in it." Samara opened the case and pulled the gown off the form. She held it up to Samara and looked at her. "It'll fit. I've always wanted to see it on a live person."

"I couldn't." Samara backed away.

"Don't worry, you won't do anything to hurt it."

Deanna didn't understand, Samara thought. "I'm not modeling wedding gowns," she explained.

"I used to love to play dress up," Deanna said as if she didn't hear Samara.

"I must be out of my mind," Samara muttered as she

found herself being helped into a century-old gown. Deanna fastened the line of buttons along Samara's back. "This is bad luck, you know."

"How can it be? My grandparents were married for sixty years. And my parents are about to celebrate their fortieth."

"My luck is always bad."

"There's no such thing as good or bad luck. You make your own luck. And maybe the gown will change your status."

"You understand that is a diametrically opposite argument? Either there is such a thing as luck and the dress could change that. Or there is no such thing as luck. It can't be both."

Deanna smiled. "You've a lawyer's mind. Justin must see that in you."

"He's never said," she said. "I mean, I don't have a lawyer's mind."

"Just logical."

"I hope," Samara said. "Justin tells me you run your own company." Samara changed the subject.

"I do. And I work damn hard to make it a success."

Deanna stood back and looked at her. Then she frowned.

"What is it?" Samara asked, thinking she must look awful.

"You need something else." Deanna turned back to the glass case. She moved to a chest next to it and opened a drawer. Pulling out a box, she opened it and removed a veil. She shook it out, then draped it over Samara's head and positioned it in her hair.

"What's this?" someone asked from the doorway.

Samara turned. Lane and Katie Beckett had come up the stairs and were standing in the doorway.

"I—" Samara began, feeling as if she'd been caught doing something wrong. She and Deanna had come up to find records, not try on someone else's heirloom.

"Doesn't she look gorgeous?" Deanna stated.

"Yes," Katie Beckett said, her voice sounding awestruck. "She does."

"If I didn't know better," Lane said, "I'd swear you were my mother on her wedding day."

Samara heard the crack in his voice.

"Dad, she's in a wedding fashion show. Maybe she could model Grandma's dress."

"Oh, no," Samara protested. "I'm only modeling bridesmaids gowns. And Geri has them already selected."

"Samara, look in the mirror," Deanna said.

Samara had seen herself once in the gown from her own trunk. She turned toward a full-length mirror that sat behind the door. The gasp that came from her when she saw her reflection was audible. She wore the entire ensemble, not just a white dress and bare feet. The veil added an ethereal quality to the reflection. It seemed that time stood still. No one said anything. She wasn't even sure they breathed. She was unaware of anything except the woman in the mirror.

It was *her*.

"What's going on up here?"

Justin joined the small group that parted to allow him access. He stopped as if suddenly frozen to the floor when he saw her.

Samara didn't see the other Becketts leave the room, but after a moment she realized she was alone with Justin.

"Your sister—" she started, then stopped.

Justin moved toward her. Time, which had stopped, started up again, but slowly. His steps where measured and easy as he moved toward her. An eternity began and ended before she was looking through the veil and into his eyes.

He lifted the veil, flipping it over her head and watching it float back over her shoulders. Her eyes followed his movements. He said nothing, only looked at her, his eyes tender and adoring. His hands reached for her shoulders and slid down her lace-covered arms until they reached her fingertips. He raised her hands and looked at her empty fingers.

"A bride should have a ring," he said in a hushed tone. He kissed her fingers.

Samara shuddered. A new emotion shot through her, something that was different from anything she'd ever felt before. Justin looked up. She cupped his face with her hands and brought it level with hers. For a moment they stared at each other, their breath mingling, their mouths only a kiss apart.

Justin's hands touched her waist. He stepped forward and kissed her. Like a groom kissing his bride in front of a congregation, his mouth touched hers in honor. His arms caressed her as if he were holding a precious artifact. But their touch was incendiary and in no time it flared into a conflagration that had them clawing at each other. Hands, arms, legs, mouths, every inch of them battled with the other as both pleasure-seeker and pleasure-giver. Ecstasy gripped her as hard as Justin's arms held her.

Never had a man affected her the way he did, taking her breath away and having her willingly give it. Never had she continued a relationship when her heart became entangled. But with Justin she kept putting it off. And this was why. This feeling. The way he made her feel, loved, protected, whole. The way his mouth felt on hers, the way he tasted, the excitement that went through her when she saw him. She liked the feel of his hands, the alignment of his body, the fire that danced through her as if some hyperactive elixir ran through her blood.

His mouth was madness on hers. She had to be mad, too, to feel so lightheaded, so alive and so good.

Their heads could have bobbed and weaved back and forth, their tongues danced and tangled for a moment or a lifetime, she didn't know. She only knew that her body was filled to the brim with rapture when his mouth moved from hers and they held each other, panting breaths as if they hadn't taken one since the time when the dress she wore was still only a bolt of fabric.

"We'd better get back downstairs," she said, her voice level, low and breathy.

"We'll have to get you out of this dress first."

Samara jumped away from him as if someone had come in and found them naked.

"You're right," he said. "Too dangerous. If I get you out of your clothes, I'm not stopping there."

Patchett's was in full swing when Samara got there. The place was usually crowded and noisy, but tonight a party appeared to be going on in one of the private rooms. The main room was having its own party.

Everyone was there when she took her seat.

"You're losing your reputation, Samara," Diana said. "We could set a clock by your actions and now look at you. Late."

"Sorry, I was held up."

"From what I hear the hold up was by a gorgeous-looking guy."

"I don't know what you mean." She feigned innocence. The truth was it wasn't Justin that made her late.

"Come now, tell 'Mama' all," Diana said.

"We all want to know," Carmen prompted.

"Don't I even get to order a drink first?"

A waiter set a glass of white wine in front of her. "We'd already ordered it. Now talk," Shane ordered.

"You can start with 'Justin Beckett is his name.'"

"That is his name. The last time I brought it up, you all were thinking I should drop him."

"Not all of us," Geri defended.

"Except Geri," Samara conceded. She brought them

up-to-date ending with the painting she was restoring. She left out the World War II bounty, and the donning of a wedding gown, although they knew she'd been to Cumberland and had dinner with his family.

"All of this isn't over a painting. Are the two of you a couple?"

Samara felt as embarrassed as a thirteen-year-old. She nodded. "We've been out a few times."

"And you've met his family? Did they like you?"

Even in the twenty-first century, it was still important that the family of the groom approve the bride and vice versa, she thought. But she wasn't a bride and there was no talk of a wedding between them.

"I wasn't there as his date. We went to look for papers."

"Did you find them?"

She shook her head.

"So what *did* you find?"

"Something Geri would be interested in." She was glad to change the subject, especially when she saw everyone perk up.

"What?" Geri asked.

"An old wedding gown."

"Another one?" Carmen said. "That's two wedding gowns. Someone is trying to tell you something."

Samara turned her head away from Carmen and looked at Geri. "The gown belonged to Justin's grandmother. They keep it in a glass case. It's beautiful."

"Do you think they would loan it to the fashion show?" Shane asked. "You could wear it."

"Actually, I was thinking of asking Geri if she'd mind me doing that very thing."

Four pairs of eyes stared at her in stunned silence. Samara lifted her wineglass and with a smile, saluted them.

Her gown was new. Justin had told Samara they were going to the Tennis Club. It wasn't a place that had anything to do with the game of tennis. It was a restaurant where people still dressed elegantly for dinner and dancing. Justin was picking her up at eight and she was putting the finishing touches on her makeup.

Her gown was purple, the strapless bodice made of horizontal folds, the skirt hanging straight to the floor. Her sandaled heels matched the dress in color. Her radiant cheeks had their own inner color.

Justin hugged her as soon as she opened the door. "You look wonderful," he said.

So did he. This was the second time she'd seen him dressed in a tuxedo and this time she was just as breathless as she had been the first time. He helped her with the wrap that matched her gown and she thought how great they looked together as they left her apartment and he helped her into his car.

The Tennis Club was nothing like Patchett's. While Patchett's was a lively, fun place, the Tennis Club had a more sedate atmosphere. It was a place for lovers and Samara felt as if she fit the bill.

After the waiter left, Justin set a small package in

front of her. It was rectangular, wrapped in black velvet paper with a gold ribbon tied around it.

"For me?" she asked, rhetorically.

He nodded.

Pulling the ribbon free, she opened the paper and then the box. Inside was a postcard. There was a huge moon window on the cover. Samara recognized it immediately.

"The White House," she said, looking up at him and then down again at the card.

The window was on the second floor of the White House, a place that was not on the public tour, but was often seen in tourist postcards and White House calendars. This one again had the vintage overtones she'd become used to associating with Justin.

On the back Justin had glued an invitation. As she read, her eyes grew large.

"The White House?" she asked. It was too incredible to believe.

Justin nodded. "Every year they hold a reception for the new staff members at EEOB."

"You are cordially invited," she read, "to attend a reception for the Presidential Staff at the White House." It went on to give the date and time.

"Will you go with me?"

"Yes," she said, elongating the word.

"It means you'll be investigated by the FBI."

She smiled slyly. "Are they going to find out you've spent several nights in my apartment? And I've spent countless nights at your house?"

He nodded. "And more."

"I'm fine with that. I have nothing to hide."

"That's not exactly true. There are some parts of you I wouldn't like them to see."

Looking at the invitation again, she asked, "May I keep this?"

"Sure, it's yours."

"I want to show it to my grandchildren some day."

"Grandchildren? For that you have to be married, don't you?"

She suddenly realized what she'd said. While being married wasn't a prerequisite for having children, it was the line along which she'd been thinking.

"Any idea who you plan for the groom?"

"I'm open to suggestions," she teased. "I'll be accepting applications next week. Are you applying for the position?"

"Yes."

Chapter 11

Sweat poured off Samara. She was on her third trip jogging around the mall. The Washington Monument pointed its needle toward the sky. The White House loomed in the background. Her clothes were soaked, her heart pounded, but its rhythm spoke with Justin's voice.

She'd been kidding, playing with the words the way she normally did when things got serious. But Justin's reply hadn't reflected the tone of the question. He *was* serious.

Samara's legs burned with the exertion. She was used to jogging. She did it every morning before going to work and on weekends. She used this track sometimes, just to vary her routine. She didn't often do more than a couple of times and today the heat index was extremely high. Stopping, she bent over, hands on her knees as she breathed in.

"Don't stop now. You need to slow your heart down."

Samara looked up. Her brother-in-law, MacKenzie Grier, stood next to her. He took her arm and they began to walk.

"Mac, what are you doing here?"

"I usually jog here during the week. Cinnamon is coming in later today. We're going to an embassy party tonight. So I came here today and found you running in this heat as if the horrors of hell were at your heels."

Had she been running that hard? She was trying to get away from Justin's answer. But no amount of running could do that.

"I didn't realize I was doing that," she said, taking a breath in between each word. "I usually jog in Meridian Hill Park. I don't even remember getting here."

"You ran all the way here from your apartment? And then around the mall several times?"

She nodded, too embarrassed to speak.

"So this is about Justin Beckett."

Samara stopped. "How did you know?"

"Samara, I'm a reporter. I know everything. And Justin called me a couple of days ago." Mac took her arm and started her walking again.

"And he told you about us?"

"He told me about a painting that you're restoring for

him. Said you believed it was one of those stolen during World War II. He asked me if there was anyone on the staff who could track down the original owner. I put him in touch with an art investigator I know."

"He did? You did?" Samara stopped again, this time with a big smile on her face.

Mac folded his arms over his chest and stood in front of her. "Now, why should that put such a huge smile on your face?"

"He was so adamant that his family owned the painting legitimately. Now he's researching its true origins."

"And that makes him an honorable man?"

She stared at her brother-in-law skeptically. "What are you saying?"

"Justin's one of the good guys. He is honorable and trustworthy and he'll always choose to do the right thing, even if the outcome isn't what he wants."

"I know," Samara said, quietly.

Justin woke but didn't open his eyes. His arms reached for Samara, but closed on empty air. His eyes flew open and he realized he'd been dreaming. She wasn't there. He was alone.

Turning over, he let out a frustrated noise. He wanted her. And she wasn't there. From his response to her joke last night, he might have scared her away for good.

He'd thought of taking her advice and giving up. Maybe that was possible a few weeks ago, but he was fully committed now. He was in love with her. Seeing her in his grandmother's wedding gown had assured him of something he'd known for weeks. The joking comment asked for a truth he couldn't deny.

Today was Saturday. She was probably working on his painting. He imagined her, dressed in jeans and a shirt covered by a smock to keep her clean while she bent over, brushing and cleaning one small area at a time.

Pushing his feet to the floor, Justin got out of bed. It had been years since he'd been able to sleep in because he wanted to and not because he was too exhausted to get up. Reaching for the phone, he quickly dialed Samara's cell-phone number.

It rang three times. After the fourth ring her voice-mail message would play and Justin would hang up without leaving one.

But she answered.

"Good morning." He smiled, excitement going through him at the sound of her voice.

"What are you doing now that you don't have to work?" she asked.

He heard traffic in the background. And a man's voice. He frowned.

"Where are you? I hear traffic."

"I'm on the mall. With Mac."

"Is something happening down there?"

"He's not tracking down a story. We met jogging. There's no emergency."

Justin realized that he may have left OEO, but his head was still there.

"I thought you'd be up in Maryland, working on the painting," Justin said.

"There's only a little left to do and Harry needed to do something else first. We're going to work on it this afternoon. It'll probably be done today or Monday night at the latest."

"I wasn't worried about that." He paused, knowing this was the lead-in to his real reason for calling. "I want to talk to you."

"That sounds serious."

Justin had to play this right. He didn't want to belittle the situation with a joke or to scare her away with a heavy explanation.

"How about we go to lunch somewhere?" He avoided the question altogether.

"I'm all sweaty and I don't have my car. Mac is going to drive me home and then I have to meet Harry. I'll call you when we're done. We'll probably be able to bring the painting back then."

He wasn't sure if she was buying time, but he accepted her terms.

"Give my best to Mac."

He replaced the receiver. What was he going to do now? The day stretched before him like a long, unrolled rug. And he wasn't used to having so much time on his hands.

Suddenly he had an idea. Something he hoped Samara would like.

* * *

She called Justin at four to let him know they were coming with the painting. It looked better than she had hoped. Harry was a wizard at what he did and she was so glad he'd taught her what he knew. She still wouldn't tackle a restoration or even a cleaning alone, but at least she knew the steps necessary to avoid further damage.

Unsure of what Justin wanted to talk about, she wondered if the art investigator had found something. Or if he wanted to discuss last night.

In her heart she knew it was about last night. She had essentially green-lighted a serious relationship. As Harry sped through the streets leading into the District, she didn't know how they would approach the subject or what she would say. Before she knew it, Harry had stopped the truck in front of Justin's house.

"We made good time getting here," she commented, trying to cover her lack of conversation during the drive. Fortunately, Harry was a quiet man and she knew he wouldn't add any weight to her lack of conversation.

Samara rang the doorbell and went back to the truck to help Harry with the new frame. Justin opened the door and quickly came out and relieved her of the burden. The painting had protective casing around the edges and they'd covered the entire package with brown paper.

They set it down on the floor of his great room and Harry pulled the strings on the paper, removing it so Justin could see the finished painting. Even though

Samara had seen it many times, this unveiling was like seeing it for the first time. It was more beautiful with multiple viewings.

Justin and Harry discussed the cleaning process, what he and Samara had done. Harry got a little technical and Justin asked questions as if he were considering a new career.

"When you transport it again," Harry instructed, "be sure to keep these protective casings on. Samara tells me it's a gift for your parents." Both men glanced at her then back at the painting. "Even if you gift wrap it, you'll still need them."

Justin agreed and Harry said goodbye to Samara. The two men headed for the door. Samara was left nervously alone. Justin's answer to her question kept coming back to her. Did he really want to marry her? Was his comment really a joke?

She paced the room like a caged lion. Then she sniffed. Something smelled good. It couldn't be coming from Justin's kitchen. He rarely ate here, he'd told her.

"This is how I imagined you," Justin said from the doorway. "Wearing jeans and a T-shirt."

She spread her arms and turned completely around, modeling the clothes for him.

"Are you cooking something?" she asked.

"I hope you're hungry."

"I am."

"I was counting on that. Let's eat."

He reached for her hand. She placed hers in his and

he led her to the kitchen. The breakfast table was empty, but several pots graced the stove. The dining-room table was set for two. Curtains had been drawn to give the room the appearance of darkness.

"I suppose you weren't planning to invite Harry for the meal."

He bent down and kissed her quickly on the mouth. "He didn't even cross my mind."

Pulling a chair out, Samara sat in it. Justin lit the candles.

"This is the first time I've had a candlelight dinner in the middle of the afternoon."

"Magic," he responded.

He left her and went to the kitchen. Coming back, he set a salad in front of her and poured her a glass of wine.

"You should have told me. I would have dressed for the occasion."

"You look beautiful as you are."

Samara dropped her head to cover the blush she was sure was on her face. Justin took a seat. He raised his wineglass and toasted her. She did the same.

"To the completion of The Wedding," he toasted.

"Completion," she said, and drank.

Justin dug into his salad. Samara watched him for a moment. He looked at her. "What is it you want to talk about?"

Samara had been nervous about the conversation all day, but she wasn't putting it off any longer.

"Last night," he said casually, as if the conversation had been about socks or something equally trivial.

"Go on."

"You asked me a question."

"I was joking."

"I know. I'd like to revoke my answer."

She blinked. "What?" It was the last thing Samara expected him to say.

"I know your feelings on marriage. I shouldn't have challenged them."

"Why did you say it then?" Samara was angry. Why should he not want to marry her? Why should he revoke his answer? Her thinking was illogical, but she didn't stop to weigh that now.

"I don't know," Justin was saying. "I saw you in that gown in our attic, and I guess I got lost in the moment."

She refused to tell him that she wasn't wearing the dress when the question came up. She had felt different in that gown, too.

"I understand. The comment about grandchildren just seemed to come out. It didn't mean anything." She was lying. It did mean something. She was confused, unsure of what was going on in her own mind.

"You should be careful not to wear another wedding gown."

Samara lifted her wineglass and drank. "I have to wear another wedding gown, at least one more time."

His eyebrows went up.

"My friend's bridal show," Samara stated.

He nodded. She'd mentioned it before.

"I was only going to wear the bridesmaid dresses, but I've committed to a gown now. Your sister called and said your parents wouldn't mind me borrowing your grandmother's dress."

Justin was quiet for a moment. "Next time I suppose I'll be prepared for it."

In the past, he'd come upon her by surprise when she was wearing the gowns.

Justin removed the salad plates and took them to the kitchen. He returned with two dinner plates. On each was a steak, baked potato and green beans.

"I didn't know you could cook." She looked up at him.

"You're looking at the extent of my culinary ability. Beyond this, I can hardly boil water."

She smiled. It seemed his trip to the kitchen closed the door on the subject of the joke and the wedding dress. For the first time since entering the house, she felt comfortable. Her shoulders dropped and she took a long breath. The rest of the meal was amiable. Samara felt as if they were getting back to where they were before yesterday.

"Would you like dessert?" Justin asked when they'd finished the meal.

"You baked, too?"

He laughed. "I told you the extent of my cooking abilities was the meal. Dessert is strictly from the German bakery down the street."

Samara put her hands on her stomach. "I don't think I have any more room."

"It's coconut custard. We can have it later."

He got up and held her chair as she stood. They went into the great room. It was still daylight outside, but the sun was setting and the room was dim. Justin went toward the light switch.

"Don't," Samara said.

He turned back and looked at her. For a long, charged moment they each appeared frozen where they stood.

"I thought," he began, "after last night, that things would be different. That you would refuse to see me again. Aren't we at the stage in relationship development where you back away?"

She hesitated. There were many ways she could have answered. Justin was easy to talk to and she'd been honest with him. "We passed that point a while ago," she said, speaking with the same volume she would if she'd been in a library.

He left his place near the light switch and came to her. Samara didn't move. She watched his easy steps until he stopped in front of her. Her eyes traveled up to his.

"Was it the point of no return?"

Samara dropped her eyes. She didn't want Justin to see anything there. Even though the light was low, she was unsure of what he might find in them. Was it the point of no return? She wasn't sure. Each time he called, her heart pounded and she couldn't wait to see him. When he didn't call, she felt depressed and longed to be with him. Her waking thoughts were of him and he occupied her dreams, too.

"Are you going to answer me?" he asked.

Still Samara said nothing. Justin put his finger under her chin and raised it until her eyes reached his.

"Can't decide?" he asked. Taking a step closer to her, he said, "Let me help you."

Justin pulled her into his arms. She came without re-sistance. He slipped his arms around her waist. His mouth settled on hers, hard, hungry, insistent. He wanted to devour her. He was devouring her. He wrapped him-self around her, drawing her to him, pulling her inward as if he needed her to be part of his makeup, part of him, inside the same skin, sharing the same heartbeat.

They mounted the stairs in each other's arms, dancing around like miniature dolls. Higher and higher they went. Fire burned around them, singeing the air, licking at their clothes. Their mouths melded and their arms linked.

He loved the feel of her skin, the warmth and smooth-ness of it. His hands ran over her, tracing the contours of her shoulders, the curve of her spine, the roundness of her bottom.

Lifting his mouth, he stared into her eyes. Desire, hot and aching gazed out at him. Love was there, too. He could see it. Yes, they had passed the point of no return.

"Each time I look at you, I get lost," he said. He kissed her eyes, then her cheeks. "I love touching you, holding you." His hands caressed her back, slowly drawing circles, descending with deliberate slowness to her hips. He could feel his erection grow against her. Excitement pooled between his legs.

Her mouth opened under his. He felt the familiar warmth pour through him, a nectar so sweet it outranked any dessert. Finding the hem of her shirt, his hands went under it. His palms touched her skin. He wanted her closer to him. He wanted the hot feel of her touch against his own naked skin.

He needed her now, wanted her in his bed. The bedroom was half a floor away, almost at the other end of the house. He didn't know if he could make it, didn't know if what pulled them together and kept them in individual bodies would allow him to get that far. Finding the hem of her shirt, he lifted it over her head. Her bra gleamed white against her skin. Unsnapping her jeans, he grabbed the zipper and slowly pulled it down. Opening it was like peeling back the door to a furnace. Heat radiated from her skin. Inch by inch as he separated the teeth, he could feel the steam of her desire being released. He touched the opening space. She was hot. His body grew harder. He didn't think it could do that. Samara melted in his arms.

He pulled her closer, his body going to heaven at the way she fit against him, the way her touch sent sparks of electricity through him. Just being in her arms was a fulfillment he hadn't thought possible.

Justin pushed her jeans down, starting at her hips, over her legs and continuing until his palms cupped the soles of her feet. Running his hands over them, he made a journey, a long, slow journey over hills and valleys that were created for his touch, for the purpose of tantalizing his sensitive skin.

He kissed her from her ankles to her stomach, running his tongue around her navel. A shudder went through her. He could feel her accelerated heartbeat and hear the hitch in her throat when his fingers encountered puckered nipples.

Anticipation welled inside him. Samara's hands skimmed across his back and down to his waist. She reached for his shirt, pulling it free from his pants, circling her hands around his waist and back. He squeezed her as sensations went through him. Starting with the buttons on the bottom of his shirt, she opened each of them, concentrating, using her hands like weapons of sexual destruction as she touched his skin under the fabric, while her mouth still worked its voodoo on him. Every molecule of his body tightened, stiffened, hardened, wanted her. Long fingernails scored his chest, seeking, traveling, working their way up and down, going through arousal points that had him bending her backward. Still she kept her hands on him, migrating to the top of his pants.

"Sam," he groaned.

Her hands met his pants zipper and conquered. Freeing him. He found the hook on her bra and pulled it away. She pushed his shirt down his arms. They undressed in a frenzy, their mouths staying together as if glued. Their hands washing over each other as if contact was as necessary as air. He pushed her against the wall, pinning her there, burying his tongue in her throat and imprinting her with his form.

Justin couldn't stand it any longer. He grabbed his pants and pulled the condom from its pocket. Quickly he sheathed himself. Samara was back in his arms the moment he finished. He lifted her. Her legs went around his waist. He pushed her against the wall and drove into her. Her back arched, holding on to him.

He was weak from his arms to his knees. Her feet slid to the floor, but the two of them remained joined in the most intimate way.

And Justin wanted them to remain that way for all time.

Chapter 12

No one truly knew how the wheels of government worked and no one could explain the volume of RSVPs for Geri's fashion show. But a week before the event, it was obvious the store would not accommodate the number of attendees. She had to move it to one of the ballrooms in Shadow Walk.

Carpenters worked night and day to setup for a different location, but on the day of the show everything was in place and ready. Everything except Geri, who was a wreck, and Samara, who couldn't believe she was preparing to let herself be dressed yet again in a wedding gown.

The show was about to start and backstage everything

was in chaos. The noise level rose and no one seemed to know where their station was or what clothes they were to wear. Nervous energy was as palpable as smoke.

"All right. That's enough," Shane shouted, clapping her hands. She stood in the middle of the room, wearing a white lace, one-piece halter-girdle straight out of a Victoria's Secret store, with matching panties. Her stockings were white and ended without support at her thighs. On her head was a long veil that made her look like one of the animated cartoon characters in an erotic magazine. "Stop all this chatter and get to the place you're supposed to be. We have a show to put on."

For a moment no one moved, then everyone scurried at once. Shane was a director and her voice left no room for argument. Geri looked relieved that someone had taken control.

Geri was to do the commentating. She had a deck of cards with the descriptions on them in her hands. Yet there was a TelePrompter set up with all the information typed and ready for her to read.

"Five minutes," she announced. "I'm going out now to begin the welcome speech." She looked at Samara. "You're first," she told her. "Get dressed."

Taking a deep breath, Samara stepped into the dress. The dresser assigned to her zipped it. The woman quickly adjusted a strand of hair that had come loose and smiled her assurance that everything was all right.

Samara went to the entryway and waited until Geri called her name. The curtain opened and she took another breath and smiled brightly. As Geri described the gown she was wearing, Samara walked the distance on the raised platform.

Her sister, Cinnamon, and her husband Mac sat at the end, to the right of the stage. Next to them were Justin and his family. Samara didn't expect them all to come. Katie Beckett smiled at her. Samara had to concentrate on her footing, making sure she didn't trip as she turned and walked back toward the curtain.

Geri described the bridesmaid's gown of yellow organza. She went through detail after detail. Samara demonstrated as she heard the different features of the gown. As she reached the curtain she was to go through, she turned back to allow the audience to see the front of the dress. They applauded and she exited.

"That was so frightening," Samara said as she returned to her dressing station. Putting her hand on her stomach, she nearly fell into the chair in front of her makeup mirror.

"No sitting down," the dresser said. "You have another gown to get into. You'll be back on before you know it."

Samara watched from the side as the others went out and came back. Shane was impressive. The stage was her element and she was completely comfortable as she floated back and forth in gown after gown. Samara went out wearing three more dresses before it was her turn to put on the first wedding gown.

It was the one from her trunk. Geri had had it cleaned and pressed and she'd added a few appliqués to give it an updated appearance.

When the curtain opened and she stood there, she heard a gasp from the direction of the room where her sister sat. Cinnamon didn't know Samara had been talked into wearing a wedding gown. It was easier now that she'd had it on more than once. The dress was beautiful and Samara felt very much like a bride wearing it. Wait until her sister saw her in Justin Beckett's grandmother's dress.

As Geri explained the features of an updated gown from the past, Samara glanced at her sister. The smile on her face was ear to ear. She smiled back. Turning, she allowed the train to fall into gentle folds. The audience watched, many of them making notes on the programs they'd been given.

Coming off stage, she grabbed the hand of one of the security guards posted there to prevent them from tripping as they walked down the three steps.

Shane glanced at Samara as she came into the dressing room. She was putting her veil on. "Here, let me help you," Samara said. She went to her and took the veil. Shane sat and Samara anchored it into her upswept hairstyle. "You look great. I can see why people cry at weddings. You must have looked like this on your own wedding day."

"Samara—"

"Shane, you're on," one of the dressers told her.

"Coming." She shrugged and rushed away.

Going before the crowd got easier each time Samara did it. She knew the majority of the audience was interested in the gown she was wearing, not her. She was merely a dress form for them to view the movement of fabric and combination of the bride's wedding day trousseau. Even with Justin looking up at her like the perfect husband, it didn't abate her comfort level.

Interspersed between the wedding gowns floating in and out of the room, Samara went through three changes of clothes suitable for bridesmaids, prom queens or summer cruises.

Finally it was time for the last gown. The right wedding dress. Samara had been buttoned and laced, her hair and makeup freshened. She was the last bride.

"Now, ladies and gentlemen." She heard Geri speaking. "These models have shown you what our new store has to offer." The audience applauded. Geri waited for the sound to stop. "But there is one more gown. Unfortunately, this one is not for sale. It's a family heirloom."

She took the time to introduce Justin's father and mother and let the audience know the gown belonged to Justin's mother.

"And now, Ms. Samara Scott in Wedding in June."

The curtain opened and for a moment Samara did not move. People stood up, applauding. Samara didn't know how Geri's crew had managed to change the stage, but there was a curved platform at the rear. All the models, wearing their final gowns, stood in a semicircle. The opening was only large enough for two more people. Interspersed between each bride was a groom. Geri had mentioned this idea once, but Samara thought she'd dropped it since none of the men were ever at a rehearsal. Still, from where she stood, they looked like a beautiful party.

Samara began her walk. Slowly, she moved through the arching brides, taking the lead and continuing to the end of the runway. Once there, she could see her sister. Cinnamon silently mouthed the words "the right wedding gown." Samara smiled, but did not acknowledge it. She looked at Katie and Lane Beckett. Tears rolled down Katie's face. Deanna handed her mother a tissue. Justin was missing.

Samara had to hold her smile in place. Where had he gone at a time like this? She turned to show the back of the dress, the long train and elegant fall of the lace. Then from out of nowhere, Justin came up the front steps and took her arm. She gazed up at him, smiling, her heart in her eyes.

"Raise the gown," he whispered. "Like in the painting."

With him supporting her, she reached down, lifted the side of the train with the hand holding her bouquet and came up extending her arm. She looked at his parents. Tears now streamed down Katie's face, but her smile was bright.

As a couple, she and Justin walked back to the semicircle and took their places, forming a portrait of brides and grooms.

The audience applauded for long moments. Geri had a huge smile on her face when she signaled them to exit.

Samara understood that the show would launch a lucrative business. Geri had the touch.

One by one the brides took a final walk on the arms of their partners before exiting the stage.

"Samara that was perfect," Shane said rushing to her as she and Justin came through the curtain. "What made you think to lift the train like that?"

She glanced at Justin. "I saw it in a picture somewhere."

He squeezed her hand and smiled.

In all her years, Samara had never known a family that seemed so genuinely happy to be with each other. But this was the Becketts. It seemed they got together for specific reasons or for no reason at all. They were still in town, staying at Justin's and today she was invited to lunch with them.

Justin had called and seemed very mysterious about there being something she needed to hear. She also had another reason for going. The wedding gown needed to be returned.

Geri had worked her magic yesterday after the show and had the dress cleaned and packed. Samara had to pick it up on her way to Justin's and she was running late. Grabbing her purse, she headed out the door and walked into the new bridal store twenty minutes later.

The place wasn't as packed as it had been last night after the show. There were a few young brides-to-be cautiously sifting through the wall of dresses. But there weren't eight models, wearing full-skirted gowns with pent-up trains, to maneuver around.

Geri had served refreshments in the store so people could browse. A few of them were back today, including Shane, whom she hadn't expected to see.

"Shane?" They hugged and said hello. "I thought you'd still be asleep."

"Geri told me you were going to be here and I wanted to talk to you. I didn't get a chance to last night."

Samara walked into the store manager's office and closed the door. She and Shane sat down at a small round table.

"What's wrong?" Samara asked. Shane was obviously distressed.

"I told the others yesterday, but I didn't want to ruin the show for you."

Samara's heart had begun to beat with fear. Shane was hesitating too long and Samara wanted to know what was wrong.

"Me? How does this affect me?"

"Your superstitions."

"What about my superstitions?" Samara didn't think of herself as being superstitious. She was a pragmatist. The others didn't see it that way. She didn't mind. There were quirks they had that she didn't understand, either.

"It's my marriage," Shane said.

"What about it?"

Shane had been married for six years. Her husband, Alex, was an actor. He was still struggling for stardom, but had gotten several bit parts in feature films. He and Shane had known each other since college.

"I'm getting a divorce," she said.

Samara's hand went to her throat. She was both relieved and saddened.

"Shane, I am so sorry." Reaching across she squeezed her friend's hand.

"It's been coming for a while. Both of us knew it. Both of us tried to ignore it." She got up and paced about the tiny room. "But our lives are taking different directions. We can't go on."

"Are you sure?" Samara asked.

"We've done everything, marriage counseling, long discussions, even greater-than-usual sex, but we're not in love any longer."

"Is there someone else?"

Shane laughed. "You would think so. He's an actor and they are notorious for having multiple partners." She paused. "But, no. There is no one else."

"What about you?" Samara kept her voice level. "Have you found someone else?"

She shook her head. "Don't mourn for me. Alex and I know this is best for us."

Samara got up and hugged her friend. "I know you're saying that. But is it really the truth? You and Alex have been together since you were in college. It has to be traumatic to separate."

"I won't lie and tell you I'm fine. I'm sure there will be nights when I'll miss him, but I'll be fine." Her eyes were a little glassy, but she smiled through them. "Don't be surprised if your phone rings in the middle of the night, some night."

"You know you can always call me."

"Well, there is the matter of Justin Beckett. Looks to me like he wants to be the one spending the night with you. Don't take my failed marriage as a reason that you shouldn't tie the knot with him."

Samara shook her head. "We have an understanding. And he knows I'm not planning to marry."

"I know them, too. And I've just told you that I'm getting divorced, but if Justin asks you, give it some thought. He looks like a man in love to me."

Samara stepped back. "It was the tux and all those wedding gowns."

"Maybe, but that might *not* be all it is. I wouldn't mind being a bridesmaid."

"You are a bridesmaid. Remember, Diana is getting married."

Shane opened the office door and looked out at the many dresses hanging along the walls. She gestured toward the bridesmaids dresses. "I can afford two gowns," she said. "I have a friend in the business."

They laughed. Shane could still make jokes. Maybe she would be all right. Most of the divorced couples she knew were doing fine. Some of them had remarried. Others had gone on to careers or work to sustain themselves as single mothers. Shane had no children.

Life was so uncertain and marriage even more. Find-

ing a person to give your whole heart to, who would
always be there, through better or worse—that had to
be the least likely event in the universe.

Lunch was a celebration. Food, conversation and
good people. Samara was glad to have a distraction after her conversation with Shane. Justin's entire family
had come, even Austin was there from Chicago and
Christian from Virginia.

"Sorry we missed your performance last night,"
Austin said. "Mom tells us you were beautiful."

"She cried," Lane Beckett said.

Samara looked at Katie and Lane Beckett.

"I never thought that dress could look better than it did
in the case," Katie said. "It only goes to show that clothes
look better on people than they do in glass cases."

"Well, I don't think we can wear it around the house,
Mom," Deanna said.

The room laughed.

"And that part at the end," Mr. Beckett said, "whose
idea was that?"

"Justin's." She gave him up immediately.

"Guilty," Justin agreed.

"What?" Micah asked. "What happened?"

"You know the painting, the one of The Wedding,
that we were looking for the papers on when Samara
first came to the house?"

Micah nodded.

"The one they had cleaned," Micah stated.

His dad nodded. "At the end of the program yesterday, Samara reached down and pulled the train of the gown out the same way it is in the painting."

"I guess this is the right time to bring this up," Justin said.

Everyone looked at him, sobering as if he was about to say something important.

"I heard from the art investigator I hired."

"And…" his father said in the pause that Justin had begun.

"And here's his report." Justin got up and pulled a folder from his briefcase that sat on a window seat near the table. Instead of giving it to his father, Justin handed it to Samara.

Surprised, she took it and opened it. There was a bill of sale inside, along with a history of the painting's previous owners.

"It's legitimately yours," she said, looking up at Lane Beckett, then switching her gaze to Justin.

"Well, I could have told you that," Lane said. "You didn't think I'd really have a painting that wasn't legally mine, did you?"

"When I saw the words on the backing, I had to be sure."

"Of course she did," Justin defended. "Samara works with rare documents. She understands how precious history is to the country and to families."

"I'm relieved it belongs to you," she said. "It's a beautiful painting, and I was honored to work on it."

"Can we see it?" Deanna asked.

"Sure," Justin said. "Samara, would you help me?"

Justin took her hand as the two of them left the room. They pulled the paper off the painting and removed the protective coverings on the ends. She began to lift her end of painting when Justin stopped her.

"There's something I want to tell them when we go back in there."

Samara stood up straight. "What?"

Justin took her hand and pulled her close. He kissed her briefly on the mouth. "That there's going to be wedding in the family. That you'll marry me."

Samara pushed herself back as if she were escaping a fire. Surprised registered on Justin's face.

"I'm sorry," she said. "I didn't mean to react so violently. But I can't marry you."

"Why? You love me. I know you. I love you. Why shouldn't we get married?"

Samara had thought of marriage to Justin. It had been there, under the surface, for months. She knew it now. But she also knew the results of marriages. They didn't last. Despite his parents only a room away, she couldn't count on it lasting forever.

"Samara, I love you. Doesn't that tell you something?"

"It tells me that I was right in the first place."

"Right about what?" Justin asked.

"About not getting involved. About not letting things go past the point of no return. About life changing us in ways we have no control over."

"Is that what you think?" he asked. "That we'll change? That you love me, but you're not willing to take a chance, believe that the two of us can defy the odds?"

"We can't. Statistics tell us that."

"To hell with statistics," he shouted. "I love you. I want to spend my life with you. I don't care about how many people get married and divorced. Or how many times they remarry. I want you. And I'm willing to try to make life everything you want it to be. Aren't you willing to do the same with me?"

Samara stared at him, mutely.

He looked at her, waiting for her to say something, for her to tell him that she loved him. Samara couldn't do it. Shane's confession was fresh in her mind. Shane had told her not to let her marriage color Samara's choices. But she couldn't. Shane's divorce only reinforced Samara's beliefs that she wouldn't be happy in the long run.

Justin stepped back. "I have my answer."

Chapter 13

"To us," Geri said raising her glass.

"To us," the others echoed, smiles all around. Glasses clinked and they drank the champagne.

"I am so glad I have friends like you," Shane said.

"I'll drink to that," Geri agreed. "I'd never have gotten though the fashion show without all of you. And I am glad to report that sales are brisk. After my mom resigned, I had to find a replacement. The manager Carmen recommended is an absolute wizard and things in my life have never been better."

"She met a man," Diana stated.

Geri blushed and sipped from her glass.

"Who is he?" Shane asked.

"He's someone I've known for years. He's an architect. We met by accident while I was working on the fashion show. He came by the store one day to speak to his brother. We had a drink and from there things got...*interesting.*"

"I am so happy for you," Shane said. Samara noticed a brightness in her eyes.

"Me, too," the others echoed.

"Samara, you're rather quiet," Shane said.

"Oh, I don't mean to be. Geri, I'm happy for you, too."

"What about you and Justin?" Carmen asked. "I thought you and Diana might be Geri's first customers."

Tears sprang to Samara's eyes before she could stop them. Only one spilled down her face. She wiped it away. The celebratory atmosphere at the table turned to that of a wake.

"Samara," Geri said, quietly. "What's happened?"

Samara took a deep breath. "Justin asked me to marry him."

"That's great," Shane shouted. Heads swiveled to stare at them. Shane's smile faded.

"Tell us what happened," Carmen prompted.

Samara explained. "He knew how I felt. How could he ask me to marry him?"

"Because he's in love with you," Diana explained. "And you're in love with him. Marriage is the natural next step."

"I'm not in love with him."

"Sorry to break this to you, sister, but yes, you are."

"What you have to do is let yourself believe it," Shane joined Diana's argument.

"You really think I'm in love with him?"

"It doesn't matter what we think," Carmen told her. "It's what you believe."

"He said he thought I was in love with him."

"What does your heart say?" Carmen asked.

Samara didn't say anything for a long time. She looked at each of her friends. Then she nodded. "I do love him."

"But you don't want to," Geri explained as if she were a psychologist. "You've told yourself so often that you don't want to join the ranks of being an ex-wife that you won't be a wife in the first place."

"I just want to be sure."

"There's no such thing," Shane said. "Life doesn't come with guarantees. The future is out of sight and always will be. If you love him, you should give him a chance."

"But, Shane, look what's happened to you. How do I know that won't happen to me?"

"You don't. And you never will. But you have to work at a relationship."

"You and Alex worked at yours, didn't you?"

"We tried—in the beginning. But as we grew, our paths moved in different directions. We're ending our marriage, but we're going to remain friends."

"Samara, you can't base your relationship on Shane's or Geri's or anyone else's," Carmen told her. "Like fingerprints, every relationship is unique. There's no blueprint, no guide, no rules. You make them up as you go

along. You build your relationship and your love the way
that it fits the two of you."

"All this sounds so logical."

"But it's not. Love is not logical. It can be miserable,"
Geri said. "But it can also be the most wonderful thing
in the world to happen to two people."

Geri's words echoed in Samara mind as she went to
work Monday morning. *Love is not logical. It can be miserable.* That she was sure of. Since she'd practically run
out of Justin's house, she'd been nothing but miserable.

She missed him. She wanted his strong arms holding
her, the feel of his mouth on hers and the magical rapture
that whisked them to their own private paradise when
they made love.

The doors to the main floor were open and the
building was coming to life for another day. Samara
entered this way instead of going to the employees' entrance. She was late. She didn't care. Sleep had eluded
her for most of the night and she had no memory of the
clock alarming. She opened her eyes and jumped out of
bed when she saw the time.

"Good morning," Alan Stackhouse greeted her as
she approached the elevator.

Samara yawned, covering her mouth with her hand.
"Good morning," she said.

"Hot date?" he teased, a knowing smile on his face.

"Not even close," she answered.

The elevator doors opened, but Samara hesitated.

She looked around, wondering, hoping that Alan was hiding a postcard for her. But his hands were empty. The doors began to close. At the last moment, he stuck his arm out and pushed them back.

"Is something wrong?"

Something was very wrong, but she wasn't about to tell him that. "I thought you might have an envelope."

He shook is head. "Justin hasn't been here in a while. I suppose his new job is keeping him pretty busy."

"I'm sure it is," she answered.

"Don't worry, when things settle down, he'll be back. He likes looking at these old documents." Alan glanced at the glass cases across the room.

"That's probably it. Justin is one to give all to his job."

Alan smiled. "You have a nice day now," he said.

"You, too, Alan." Samara stepped into the small room and Alan released the doors. The moment they closed she slumped against the wall. She wanted a sign, something from Justin that said they could get back together, but not marry.

But Justin wasn't that kind of man. He wanted to marry her. He was from a large, loving family, and he wanted to replicate that life in his own right. Why had he chosen her? Samara couldn't answer that. She'd told him time and again that she wasn't ever marrying.

Yet, were her actions speaking that language? She shook her head as if she'd voiced the question aloud. She'd run into his arms whenever he came. She sought him out and wanted to be with him, spend time, talk, get to know him. Why hadn't she thought where that would lead? Why hadn't she stopped it when she could?

"And when was that?" she asked the air.

Taking the job at EEOB was probably a lifesaver, Justin thought. At OEO, lives were in his hands. He had to be on point at all times. He couldn't have his concentration broken for even a moment. And Samara did more than break his concentration.

Like now, she was at the forefront of his mind. While he was supposed to be reading through the miles of litigation on his desk, working out the details and constitutional implications of the opposition, he was thinking of how beautiful her eyes looked when she smiled.

He had to get out of the building. Maybe a walk along Pennsylvania Avenue would clear his mind. In the past he'd used the Archives building for that purpose. He wouldn't go within a mile of it now.

Few people ever walked through the front doors of the EEOB. They used the tunnels to get to the White House next door or headed through one of the entrances that led to the parking lot. Justin pushed the glass doors open and stepped onto the top flat stone. The entrance was like a giant picture frame.

Heading past the White House and Treasury Department, he looked across the street at the park where he'd once waited for Samara to come along. She wasn't there today and not likely to be. It was only past noon. She would be below ground, lost in her documents and books, not thinking of him or the bereft way she'd left him.

Stopping at the light on the corner of Fifteenth Street where Pennsylvania and State Place NW intersected, he waited with the crowd to cross. It was a warm day and the tourists were out in force. But Justin's eyes honed in on the one person standing across the street.

Samara!

She stood on the New York side while he was on Pennsylvania. What was she doing there? The Archives building was blocks away. In a moment, her eyes connected with his. He saw her body stiffen, saw her take a deep breath and hold it. The light turned green and everyone moved except them. She stayed on New York, he on Pennsylvania.

He knew they had to run into each other sooner or later. The District had over a million people counting commuters in the sixty-eight-square-mile tract, but eventually they had to run into each other. Justin didn't think it would be this soon. Bracing himself, he waited while she left New York Avenue and walked to Pennsylvania.

"Hello," she said with a smile.

"You're a long way from work," he said without greeting.

"It's not that far," she said, glancing over her shoulder.

The crowd gathered as the light turned red. Justin and Samara moved back, near the gate of the Treasury Department, to get out of the flow of people.

"I'm glad I ran into you," she said.

Justin thought her voice sounded very formal, as if they were two acquaintances who hadn't met in a while, but had a secret to share. Yet they were former lovers, and the former was barely a day old. He could still imagine her imprinted on him and hear her howls as they both climaxed at the same time.

"I wanted to apologize for the other day. I know it was rude of me to act so strangely when you asked me…" She stopped, swallowing and looking uncomfortable.

She seemed to have a hard time saying the words. "When I asked you to marry me," he supplied.

She nodded, still refusing to utter the words.

"I know my actions led you to think—"

"Samara," he interrupted. "I love you. But I'll survive," he said. He would survive, but he would never stop loving her. He'd learn to live with the pain. This feeling had happened to him before. Eventually it would dull, but not die. And the ordeal he had to go through to get past the learning process would be like scaling a glass mountain that had oil running down its sides.

"Justin." She reached up to touch his face. He jumped back as if she were about to deliver a blow to his head. Her hand fell to her side.

He shouldn't have done that. It was a reflexive action, one of self-preservation. He couldn't let her touch him. He knew if she did he'd lose it. She looked so fresh and beautiful with the sun in her hair and the light on her face.

He'd have swept her into his arms and let the spectators of the nation's capital have a good look at a man in love.

Samara had interpreted the action differently. Her words told him that. "I'm sorry," she said. "I won't bother you again."

He watched her walking away. It took every ounce of resolve he had not to run after her, fall on his knees and beg her to come back. But he couldn't. He knew he couldn't. He also knew she was in love with him. But she had to discover it. She had to be the one to believe that they could take the next step and all they believed in wouldn't fall apart.

He only hoped she would find out before time and distance separated them forever.

Samara refused to cry. There was nothing to cry for. She'd chosen this direction. Why should she feel anything except satisfaction at achieving her goal? Yet she did. She knew she wanted Justin, but it was too late. When she saw him standing on the corner, her heart nearly jumped through her chest, but he'd moved on.

She thought it would take a little longer than a few days. He'd said he loved her. That had to be a lie. If he loved her, how could he jump away from her hand like that? How could he tell her he was going to get over her, that he would survive without her?

Wasn't that what she wanted? She was confused. Justin said one thing and did another. Well, she could do it, too. She could get over him. Squaring her shoulders, she continued up Sixteenth Street, refusing to look over her shoulder, although the effort not to was greater than lifting a 747.

"It's not working," Samara told Carmen as they looked through the items that would soon be up for auction.

"See anything you want to bid on?" she asked.

"I'm not talking about bidding, and you know it."

Carmen turned to her, looking her straight in the eye. It was her jury look. Samara recognized it.

"Are you in love with him?" she asked.

Feeling as if she were under oath, Samara answered truthfully. "Yes." The single word rebounded in her mind. It was the first time she'd said it out loud. Suddenly the weight she hadn't realized she was carrying lifted. She felt lighter. She was in love with him.

"Then tell him. It will change your world. And it'll put him out of the misery he's in."

Samara stood looking down at a trunk. "I think it's too late for that." Carmen listened intently as Samara related the events that took place in front of the Treasury Department.

"That was his method of protecting himself. We all do it, throw up walls around ourselves when we feel our emotions may be hurt or destroyed. Men are worse than women."

Samara wondered if that was true. Had what happened with Justin been his way of protecting himself?

"Should I bid on the trunk again?" Carmen asked.

"What?" Samara asked.

"The trunk?" She pointed to the beat-up trunk they were standing in front of. It looked as if it had been in someone's attic for a hundred years.

Samara remembered Justin's trunk. It looked as if it had been around the world. "No," she said. "Look at the luck I had the last time I bought a trunk." Samara walked away from it. The signal sounded that the auction was about to begin.

"Better take our seats," Carmen said.

Samara followed her friend. Samara sat down. She looked at the empty seat beside her. The last time she came to an auction, Justin had been in the seat next to hers. They weren't at Shadow Walk and she didn't expect to see him here this time. Moments later a young girl in her early twenties with bouncing blond hair slipped into the seat. Irrationally, Samara wanted to ask her to move, tell her that the seat was taken. But she turned around and focused her attention on the auctioneer.

Samara's mind wasn't on the auction. Should she tell Justin how she felt? Could she? Could she even get close enough to him to speak? The last time had been a disaster.

But the next time, she told herself. The next time would be different.

Cinnamon had given Samara the idea, but it was Diana that worked out the details. She'd send him a postcard. It had worked for him. Why shouldn't it work for her? For them?

Samara held the card in her hand, looking down at the wonder of modern computer graphics and a creative mind. It was the scene from the painting, only this one had her as the bride and Justin as the groom.

Anyone who was anyone in the District had a photo somewhere, on the Internet, in a newspaper morgue, uploaded to Facebook or one of the other personal web services. Diana had found several of Justin.

Using the wedding gown from the now infamous trunk, the one item that had started her on this railroad to Justin, Samara had dressed in it and a photographer had taken several pictures. Using the magic of the computer, Diana had combined all the photos to compose a replica of them in the appropriate pose.

For a moment Samara's eyes misted, like a veil taking her back to three nights ago. Three sleepless nights. She'd admitted to herself that she was in love with Justin. But she hadn't admitted that she wanted to do anything about it. Not take the lead and aggressively approach him. She thought the next time she ran into him she'd be more prepared for the onslaught of feelings that ripped through her. She would be able to control the memory of him and how they had been together. But in the dawning of the day, when the sun blushed the horizon like red wine spilling on a white carpet, she understood that she would never be the same again. That her life was linked to his with a bond that was strong. She could never be prepared to love someone and watch him walk away.

She had to do something. He had pursued her, broken through her defenses, defied her attempts to stay away from him, and challenged her to fall in love.

And he'd succeeded.

All too well, she thought.

Deep in places that couldn't be viewed through the most powerful microscopes, embedded in her DNA was a love so strong that the thought of never seeing Justin again caused physical pain.

Samara hoped it wasn't too late, that she hadn't killed the love Justin had for her. She had to know if there was still a chance. She had to swallow all the words she'd said and nakedly beg him to love her.

She looked down at the postcard again, gauging its effectiveness and the distance to Justin's front door. She hadn't called. She didn't know if he was home, but she had to try something. She had to take a chance. She believed in him, and she believed in herself. In them. As a couple. She believed in the fate that had brought them together and that she could take a leap of faith, that she could repair the rift she had torn in their relationship.

Giving herself no time to change her mind, she walked directly to the door and punched the doorbell. It reverberated inside, but Justin didn't immediately answer the door. Tapping her toe on the wooden porch and biting on her lower lip, she rang the bell a second time.

The door opened. Justin stood there. Samara's breath caught in her throat. She wasn't sure which one of them was more surprised.

Justin's eyes opened wider when he saw her. He wore only a pair of jeans and an open shirt that looked like he'd grabbed it on his way to the door. He hadn't shaved in several days by the look of him and by the puffiness around his eyes he hadn't slept in the same amount of time.

Had she done this to him?

"What do you want?" he asked. His voice was gruff. Samara was pushed back by it. She felt the wall of protection rise and she suppressed the need to turn and run.

She wasn't running this time. This time he had to turn *her* away.

"Well, you obviously have something to say. Are you planning to say it or just stand there?"

Her voice deserted her. But her heart told her she loved him. And love was worth sacrificing her pride for. Justin was worth it.

He stood back, opening the door in a gesture of exaggerated welcome. Samara stepped back, extending her arm and offering him the postcard.

He looked at her hand, at the photo that Diana had layered image upon image to create the effect of a single merged picture. It showed the way her love had grown, not by huge degrees, but by small layers that built one atop the other. It was how she knew their lives could be, building one day at a time. She had to have that chance.

Justin took the card, staring at the photo. Bringing it closer to his face, he scrutinized the picture.

"Turn it over," Samara said, uttering the first words since Justin opened the door.

He turned the card over and read the back. Looking up at her, he read aloud, "I'll take the chance, but only with you. Will you marry me?"

He stopped, staring at her, waiting for her to say something.

"You have to say it out loud," he said.

She swallowed. "I—I love you," she said. The words hadn't stuck in her throat, although fear that he would reject her had made her stutter. "I love you. I want to marry you. I want to spend my life with you."

Justin didn't seem to have heard her. She waited for what seemed like an eternity. He said nothing, didn't move from his place inside the door. Fear grew inside her. She was too late. He didn't believe her.

Then he moved. She didn't see it, his strike was as fast as lightning. He pulled her through the door, closed it, backed her against it and kissed her. His mouth devoured hers. The kiss felt like they had been separated for decades and only now discovered each other, discovered their love as shiny as a newly minted coin.

"I love you," she whispered against his lips. "I've always loved you. I'll always love you."

"And you'll marry me?"

She smiled, feeling happiness rush through her. It shot through her bloodstream, a narcotic more powerful than any known drug. "Yes, yes," she cried. "I'll marry you, have your children, live in the suburbs, live in the city, go to parties, scream at you, fight with you, listen to your stories, laugh at your jokes, make up, make love."

The Right Wedding Gown

"For all time?" he asked.

"As long as day dawns and night falls."

"You are incredible," he said. He took her hand and led her into the great room. He sat on the sofa and pulled her onto his lap.

"I know this might seem like a surprise," she said.

"I've known all along," he told her. "I was waiting for you to find out." He kissed her neck. Spasms of love and need flooded inside her.

"I'm so glad I did. I realized that living without you made me so miserable that I'd die without seeing you."

"I thought I was going to die, too. When I saw you that day and you tried to touch me, it was all I could do not to crush you against that fence. But you needed to find out for yourself. Samara, I love you. But love doesn't come with guarantees."

"I know that now," she told him. "But if we work at it, it can last a lifetime." She kissed him tenderly. "I'm willing to work as hard as possible. You have my promise."

"You have more than that," he said. "You have my love and I'll never let you forget it."

He kissed her again. The postcard slipped to the floor, unseen by either of them, but reflecting the layers of their life and love, strong enough to defy all odds.

REQUEST YOUR FREE BOOKS!

2 FREE NOVELS
PLUS 2 FREE GIFTS!

KIMANI ROMANCE™

Love's ultimate destination!

YES! Please send me 2 FREE Kimani™ Romance novels and my 2 FREE gifts (gifts are worth about $10). After receiving them, if I don't wish to receive any more books, I can return the shipping statement marked "cancel." If I don't cancel, I will receive 4 brand-new novels every month and be billed just $4.69 per book in the U.S. or $5.24 per book in Canada. That's a savings of over 20% off the cover price. It's quite a bargain! Shipping and handling is just 50¢ per book.* I understand that accepting the 2 free books and gifts places me under no obligation to buy anything. I can always return a shipment and cancel at any time. Even if I never buy another book from Kimani Press, the two free books and gifts are mine to keep forever.

168 XDN EYQG   368 XDN EYQS

Name	(PLEASE PRINT)	
Address		Apt. #
City	State/Prov.	Zip/Postal Code

Signature (if under 18, a parent or guardian must sign)

Mail to **The Reader Service:**
IN U.S.A.: P.O. Box 1867, Buffalo, NY 14240-1867
IN CANADA: P.O. Box 609, Fort Erie, Ontario L2A 5X3

Not valid to current subscribers of Kimani Romance books.

Want to try two free books from another line?
Call 1-800-873-8635 or visit www.morefreebooks.com.

* Terms and prices subject to change without notice. Prices do not include applicable taxes. Sales tax applicable in N.Y. Canadian residents will be charged applicable provincial taxes and GST. Offer not valid in Quebec. This offer is limited to one order per household. All orders subject to approval. Credit or debit balances in a customer's account(s) may be offset by any other outstanding balance owed by or to the customer. Please allow 4 to 6 weeks for delivery. Offer available while quantities last.

Your Privacy: Kimani Press is committed to protecting your privacy. Our Privacy Policy is available online at www.eHarlequin.com or upon request from the Reader Service. From time to time we make our lists of customers available to reputable third parties who may have a product or service of interest to you. If you would prefer we not share your name and address, please check here. ☐

NATIONAL BESTSELLING AUTHOR

ROCHELLE ALERS

INVITES YOU TO MEET THE BEST MEN...

Close friends Kyle, Duncan and Ivan have become rich, successful co-owners of a beautiful Harlem brownstone. But they lack the perfect women to share their lives with—until true love transforms them into grooms-to-be....

Man of Fate
June 2009

Man of Fortune
July 2009

Man of Fantasy
August 2009

ARABESQUE®

www.kimanipress.com
www.myspace.com/kimanipress

KPRABMSP